THE VIEWING ROOM

FLANNERY
O'CONNOR
AWARD
FOR
SHORT
FICTION

Nancy Zafris,
Series Editor

The Viewing Room STORIES BY JACQUELIN GORMAN

THE UNIVERSITY OF GEORGIA PRESS   ATHENS

"Ghost Dance" was first published in *Slake: Los Angeles*, issue 2,
"Crossing Over." It is reprinted with permission.

Paperback edition, 2017
Published by the University of Georgia Press
Athens, Georgia 30602
www.ugapress.org
© 2013 by Jacquelin Gorman
All rights reserved
Designed by Kaelin Chappell Broaddus
Set in by 10.7/14 Dante MT Std by Graphic Composition, Inc., Bogart, Georgia

Most University of Georgia Press titles are
available from popular e-book vendors.

Printed digitally

The Library of Congress has cataloged the
hardcover edition of this book as follows:

Gorman, Jacquelin, 1955–
[Short stories. Selections]
The viewing room : stories / by Jacquelin Gorman.
xii, 136 pages ; 23 cm.
"Winner of the Flannery O'Connor Award for Short Fiction."
ISBN-13: 978-0-8203-4548-2 (hardcover : alk. paper)
ISBN-10: 0-8203-4548-2 (hardcover : alk. paper)
I. Gorman, Jacquelin, 1955– Viewing room: April. II. Title.
PS3557.O7597V54 2013
813'.54—dc23
2013003109

Paperback ISBN 978-0-8203-5145-2

For My Children

Understanding, she explains, can only come to pass
when all banned truths, even those of the poor, the
ugly, the enraged, the contaminated, the maimed,
the contagious, the marked, the perverted,
return fully to earth.
And understanding, she cautions,
is a fragment of love.

JULIE BRICKMAN,
What Birds Can Only Whisper

Think occasionally of the suffering,
of which you spare yourself the sight.

ALBERT SCHWEITZER

[CONTENTS]

[ACKNOWLEDGMENTS]

First, I owe a great debt of gratitude to the magnificent Flannery O'Connor for being absolutely fearless in every aspect of her life. The editorial staff at University of Georgia Press are worthy preservers of her legacy. Thank you, Nancy Zafris, Jane Kobres, and Sydney DuPre for your invaluable assistance in getting these stories into the best possible shape for public viewing.

This collection began its life in the nurturing incubator of the Spalding University Brief Residency MFA Program in Louisville, Kentucky. Thank you, Sena Jeter Naslund, Karen Mann, and Kathleen Driskell for its creation, and thank you, Alice Bingham Gorman for inspiring me to go to there and cheering me on all along the way. The constant faith of my mentors and workshop leaders kept this book alive though many drafts and revisions; Mary Yukari Waters, Julie Brickman, Robin Lippincott, Richard Goodman, Kenny Cook, Crystal Wilkinson, Kirby Gann, and Eleanor Morse.

Writing is unbearably lonely, and I would not have survived to tell any of these tales without my two families of fellow writers; my first Los Angeles writing group, Rita Williams, Victoria Pynchon, Russel Lunday, Birute Putrius Keblinskas, Kathleen Wakefield, Barry Le-Mesurier, Jan Bramlett, Peter Nason, and our lost soul, Jonathan Aurthur. And my second writing family, the Spalding TB3 group, Writing Warrior Women, Julie Stewart, Bridgett Jensen, Cindy Corpier, Lia Eastep, Lori Reisenbichler, and Katy Yocum.

I am grateful that my literary agent, Jim Levine, who launched this publishing journey with my memoir many years ago, is still in my corner.

I was thrilled to have a version of "Ghost Dance" published in *Slake Magazine* No. 2, "Crossing Over," and my endless admiration to the editors, Joe Donnelly and Laurie Ochoa for their extraordinary contribution to the literary community of Los Angeles. Additionally, I am honored that Kaaren Kitchell of the *TheScreamOnline*, published a version of "Passerby," David Lynn of the *Kenyon Review* published a version of "Blood Rules," and Alex Fabizio of *The Journal* published a version of "The Law of Looking Out for One Another."

And thank you to all the patients and their families at UCLA medical centers in Westwood and Santa Monica who allowed me to share such sacred space—although never named or referenced by any facts in these stories, you gave this book its heart.

And thank you to Sister Colleen Harris, and all the wonderful people at Blessed Sacrament Social Services in Hollywood, for the sanctuary of the Quiet Room, where I spent an amazing year dining with homeless friends, and the Passerby, who called for help when I fell into his hidden world, and saved my life.

Thank you to NAMI (National Alliance on Mental Illness), and Sharon Dunas, MFT, and Lois and Sam Bloom, and all the remarkable people who fight to erase the stigma of brain disorders, to prevent suicide, and to support families who must cope with the devastation of mental illness in their loved ones. You are my heroes.

And to Donate Life of California, for welcoming me into the Organ Transplantation Community and teaching me that life is a gift, to be given many more times than received.

And to my dear friend, an adored chaplain and human rights advocate, Michael Louis Eselun—you gave this book its soul. Thank you, Michael, for the spiritual lives you keep saving, including mine, over and over again.

And, finally, to my family—my sisters, Polly, Sally, and Mary Clark, and my daughter, Kelsey, and my son, Ben, thank you for lighting my way through the darkest times.

I love you all, heart, mind and soul.

THE VIEWING ROOM

The Viewing Room APRIL

In every large urban hospital, there is a viewing room, designated for family and friends to look upon the dead one more time. The viewing room is the same size and shape as the other patient rooms, with one notable exception. There is no window to the outside world. This is a room with an interior view toward its center, where the body lies on a hospital bed, at a raised height, like a stage. It is a standard-issue hospital bed stripped down to its essence, without all the amenities for living patients, such as televisions, call buttons, eating trays, telephones, pillows, and oxygen.

A private bathroom is connected to the viewing room, with shelves and cabinets filled with cleaning supplies. These supplies are not for cleaning up the dead. The body, by the time it arrives here, is always freshly washed, disconnected from all life-support devices, devoid of color; each of its open orifices has been thoroughly rinsed, sanitized, and tightly sutured shut. The bodily fluids of the living, those who come here to mourn the dead, are far more difficult to contain. The wounds of the grievers are active wounds, bleeding, highly contagious, and receptive to further contamination and always seeping with live bacteria.

Upon viewing their beloved dead, the bodies of the people who come here overflow with emotion. They flood tears and mucus; they vomit profusely, usually missing the small plastic bowls or towels provided. They rip open their clothes to tear at their skin or pull out their hair until they bleed. They pound their heads against the white walls, leaving marks, even indentations. They press their damp, bruised cheeks against the newly slick but always cool and strangely comforting linoleum floor, spreading the germs in this circular way, head to toe and back up again.

It is strict hospital policy never to leave a visitor alone with the body in the viewing room. Only authorized hospital personnel with universal access badges may be present during a viewing, and only two departments have cards and codes to every room in the hospital—Janitorial Services and Spiritual Care. At first glance, there seems to be little connection between these two. And yet over the years their cleanup work continues to dovetail in many areas—the morgue, the operating room, the recovery room, the emergency room, family waiting rooms—but none more than the viewing room. Motion-activated surveillance equipment continuously documents what happens here, leaving a permanent record of what the living do when they choose to share this closed-in space with the dead.

[THE LAW OF LOOKING OUT FOR ONE ANOTHER]

Henrietta was fifteen minutes late for her first all-night shift alone as the hospital chaplain. In another fifteen minutes, the Spiritual Care Department chair would be notified and she could lose her privilege to be on the on-call list. She had been training for this job for three months, shadowing the staff, learning to handle all sorts of emergencies, as an intern without pay, and now it was an ordinary traffic jam that was going to take it all away. Ordinary, at least, for the west side of Los Angeles. A caravan of ambulances had screeched ahead of her on Wilshire Boulevard and now blocked the way into the UCLA Medical Center's main parking lot. Henrietta bowed her head in allegiance to the sound of the sirens—a childhood reflex—praying for the hurt people inside, their families, the paramedics, and finally the hospital staff, including herself, a spiritual family privileged to heal their wounds.

This had started as a family ritual. At the sound of an ambulance siren's wail, her mother would slow the car down, pull off to the side of the road, and stop the engine cold. Then she would hold out her hands to hold her children, crushed soft tissues flapping through her fingers like prayer flags. She would remind God, ever so politely, "Please pay extra attention to those suffering strangers, and all their caregivers right now, this very minute, and thank you very kindly in advance."

She had never wavered. "It *is* the law," she would solemnly tell Henrietta and her two sisters, when their heads had popped up too quickly and she had caught them looking before the sound had died down. "And I could, the responsible driver, with precious burdens in this car, get a ticket for not following it—many points and a large fine," she would add, squeezing their hands hard as one last emphasis.

Henrietta had believed her, of course. It was not until she took her written driver's license exam that she had found out that the motor vehicle laws were not so generous-hearted, that the maximum effort required of a driver was to attempt to slow down and get out of the way of the speeding ambulance to prevent accidents.

"Well, it should be the law for my children," her mother had replied when Henrietta had confronted her. "It is the law of looking out for one another."

This had been Henrietta's introduction to group intercessory prayer in that mobile confessional, the family station wagon, as it evolved into a makeshift roadside chapel. They had never dared break their mother's commandment to hold hands with one another, whether they wanted to or not, hated each other or not, three girls and the adored baby brother, always fighting for that most treasured battle turf, the front passenger seat by the window. They had sat obediently, sighing loudly and dramatically their only protestation, but always offering up their hands, forming a soft, warm circle of humanity inside the hard metal rectangle. Through many years, they had gone on family vacations this way, round and round, in a seemingly endless series of prayer circles, until they had turned beyond the comforting straight line of childhood, curving around the dangerous, surly U-turn of adolescence, back again to the familiar friendship with one another as adults, one sister older than Henrietta, one sister younger, but all adults.

Had they prayed enough times to make any difference? Did her mother know now—or did God with His panoramic vision know back then—that despite all their generous prayers for others, their own magic circle would be broken? Her mother had outlived her only son yet was not there to hold him when he had been dying, not even within the siren's range of a prayer. It had been his accidental killer who had held him, a distraught stranger, whispering words of reassurance, of apology, holding him close in his arms, flesh against flesh, heart against heart. "Not alone," her mother would repeat later, like a calming mantra. "At least my son did not die alone."

Henrietta bowed her head one last time at the steering wheel altar before she left the car. She no longer prayed the way her mother had taught her, the way they all used to pray together before her brother was killed. She didn't pray for other people first anymore. She prayed more economically and efficiently, starting with a prayer for herself at the center of the circle and then praying her way out to the others.

"Please, God, don't let me be too late for work," was her first prayer as the hospital front doors opened. Her on-call shift had started ten minutes ago, at 5:30, and there was only a half-hour grace period where the day chaplain could report on open cases.

The day-shift chaplain, Maurice, looked up as Henrietta came through the door.

"Finally!" He tilted his dimpled chin toward the gigantic clock that covered one entire wall of the office, its second hand ticking loudly and relentlessly, as if it had been taken from a nineteenth-century train station but still remembered its past importance. Maurice was impeccably dressed and looked wonderfully fresh after eight hours of work. He always looked as if he could handle any possible contingency, the full spectrum, the "carry, marry, bury" cycle of ceremonies, with a showman's style. Henrietta had heard that he had once had a successful career as a professional ice dancer.

"I was just on my way to the Neonatal Unit for an emergency baptism. Now you'll have to do it. I don't have that kind of time," he sighed. "All yours, my dear." He handed her a clear sandwich-sized baggie. She could see a tiny white satin hat, a scrolled-up piece of paper, a plastic white rosary necklace, and a vial of holy water.

Maurice's back was turned away from her. He was sliding the magnetic button beside his name from the on-call column to the out-of-range column.

She touched him lightly between the shoulder blades, and he spun around.

"Wait, Maurice, please. I know I'm late, and you need to leave. And I'm sorry, but I can't do this without some help. I'm not Catholic, you know."

"So?"

"I can't do a Catholic baptism. I'm a minister, not a priest."

"Yes, I already gathered that much." He waited, grinning at her.

"But it's not the same kind of . . ."

"Oh, for God's sake, please spare me the personal details. All that doesn't matter here," he interrupted, his smile vanishing. "Haven't you read the on-call manual? You don't need to be anything—not Catholic, not ordained, not even flying around with angel wings. In fact, it's not about you, my dear."

He faced her and looked at her closely for the first time. His eyes were deep-set, huge, pale green, and hauntingly beautiful.

"It's the situation, not your credentials, that gives you the authority to baptize," he said.

"Situation?"

"Oh, for Christ's sake! Why do I always get the newbies?" He shook his head. "Dying Infant Exception. All chaplains can baptize babies who have no chance of making it out of here."

Henrietta stood there, staring at him, her hands clenched around the plastic baptism kit.

"I can't see how I can do this. I'm sorry. It's just too much."

"Please don't tell me . . . this is your first dead baby?"

"Well, yes," she confessed. "Of course, I've done baptisms but never like . . ."

"I know, I know," he said, fluttering his perfectly manicured fingers at her. "You have only baptized those lucky babies that get to grow up. Oh, well, better put that all out of your mind right now. It's a horse of a different color here. Think of this as a twofer sacrament. You are baptizing the spirit and commending it to God all in one fell swoop, so they say. It can be a very healing moment in its own weird way, really, you'd be surprised . . ."

"I've had enough surprises," she said.

He flashed her a radiant smile. "Oh, now, honey, don't be saying that. The night is still young." He looked at his watch, sighing dramatically. "All right. I can give you fifteen minutes. That's all. I'll walk you up there and I'll brief you on the way, but I'm sneaking down the back elevators to the parking garage before those nurses see me. They just love me up there. And like I said, I just don't have that kind of time."

He disappeared out the door. She caught a glimpse of him skating down the corridor to the staff elevators and ran after him.

"Here's the deal. If you don't remember anything else, at least remember this . . ." His voice trailed off. And then he turned a corner.

When she finally caught up to him, he let her take his arm, as if they were dancing partners. He was whispering now so that the others waiting for the elevator could not hear him, but it came out more like an ominous hiss.

"Vital stats—listen up. Single mom—barely legal age and not married to the dad. Baby's got to have her mom's last name on the certificate, ok? They're sticklers here for that stuff now that we're up for accreditation this year. You can put down the first name Bozo for all they care, but only Mom's last name—got it?"

"Got it. Are both parents up there?"

He slowed down as they left the elevator on the fifth floor and patted the hand that was gripping his arm. His skin was soft; his thumb rubbing her skin was gentle, familiar, not sexual, not sensuous, but intimate, as if it were her own hand.

"All right, I might as well give you the bad news first. Dad and

Mom are not together at all—crappy deal, believe me, these babies having babies. Anyway, keep them apart at all costs. Mom's up in the unit right now. She's the Catholic. But as soon as that baby dies, you need to bring the body to the viewing room for Dad's turn to say good-bye."

Now she understood why Maurice had been so relieved to see her show up to take over the shift. "Maurice, I don't think I can do this by myself. Could you . . ."

He stopped moving and pulled his arm away.

"Stay later? Not on your life." He laughed, as if the question were preposterous. "I know how to set my boundaries. I am my own Border Patrol, my dear. And nobody makes me cross the date line. Theater date, that is. And speaking of that . . . you'd better keep your own clock running. Make it short and sweet . . . you should have that baby baptized, viewed, and at the morgue inside an hour from now."

"You're kidding! An hour?"

He smiled at her. "Even less, if you can manage it. Believe me. Every minute in there will seem like an eternity to you and a blink of an eye to them." He frowned. "Or the other way around, but you get my point." Again, he looked at his watch. "Well, my dear, don't worry. You'll be fine. Listen, I really do have to go. It's already six— curtains up at eight." He winked at her as he back-stepped into the elevator, waving good-bye.

Henrietta slid the plastic bag into her pocket next to her portable Book of Worship as she headed toward the Neonatal Intensive Care Unit. She looked down at the case status report and tried to decipher Maurice's tiny, perfect print handwriting as she walked. As it turned out, she did not need to look at the paper to find the room.

She could hear the mother singing. What was it? A hymn? No. But something very familiar. And then she recognized it—a song her mother used to sing to her.

> *Baby's boat's a silver moon,*
> *Sailing o'er the sky,*
> *Sailing o'er a sea of dreams,*
> *As the clouds roll by . . .*
>
> *Sail, baby, sail*
> *Out across the sea*
> *Only don't forget to sail*
> *Back again to me . . .*

It was a lullaby for singing a child to sleep, but Henrietta had never heard the wrenching plea in the refrain until this moment.

She leaned back against the nurses' console and closed her eyes, trying to remember the second verse. It drifted back to her, and she entered the room singing the words softly.

> *Baby's fishing for a dream,*
> *Fishing near and far.*
> *His line a silver moonbeam is,*
> *His bait a silver star.*

She could see the back of an oily blonde ponytail bobbing up and down as she entered the room. Henrietta moved past an incubator. It was empty. All the machines were next to it, all the tubes inside, but the monitors were blank, shut down, and only bloody bandages were on the floor under them. There were snapshots of an infant taped all around the inside of the incubator. Henrietta was struck by how healthy the baby looked, plump, a huge gummy smile. She couldn't tell the baby's gender by the photos. There was one of the baby in a bunny costume holding a tiny Easter basket. It was only the second week in April. The baby's illness must have moved fast.

She walked over to stand in front of the rocking chair and was startled by what she saw. The mother was a young teenager, with fresh acne on her cheeks. She looked up, tears glistening in her eyes, which were a pale, washed-out blue, almost an exact match to the faded blue in the flannel blankets of the swaddled shape she held against her chest. She leaned over and grabbed Henrietta's hand. Unlike Maurice's, her touch was both rough and clinging.

"Sing more, please," she begged. "Nobody else would sing with me. It's his favorite."

Henrietta nodded and sat on the floor beside the girl's feet, which were in sandals, bright pink with butterflies at the opening between the toes—the kind of sandals Henrietta's four-year-old niece wore.

> *Sail, baby, sail*
> *Out across the sea*
> *Only don't forget to sail*
> *Back again to me.*

A nurse, standing in the corner of the room, waited until the refrain was done and then cleared her throat loudly.

"Lacey, this is Henrietta, our hospital chaplain. She has come to baptize your baby, all right? Just like we said, right?" Only the lilting Jamaican accent and her huge liquid amber eyes, filled with tears, warmed the nurse's chilling words.

Lacey clutched her son close, her head bent over his body. Then she started to wail, her body rocking back while the chair squeaked loudly on the floor.

Henrietta stood up suddenly, her knees aching, almost letting out a wail herself. She walked around behind Lacey and put her arms gently around both of them. A tiny foot popped out of the bottom of the blanket. Instinctively, Henrietta reached down to caress it. The foot was cold as ice. The baby had not survived long without the machines. How much longer before Lacey realized her baby had died?

Suddenly, Lacey sat up straight and stopped rocking. She looked at Henrietta. "Want to see him?"

Henrietta knew that she could not pause. She nodded and lifted the covers away, praying that she could look without noticeably flinching. She was relieved to see that his skin had retained some color, was not yet dusky gray. His hair sparkled synthetically, like doll's hair, gold filigree wisps around his face, a shiny small circle of light in his child-mother's arms.

"He's beautiful," Henrietta said.

"Yes, he is," Lacey answered, tugging the baby's hair playfully into a point above his head, making him look like a troll doll. His head did not flop, did not move an inch, the neck already stiff. They were running out of time. Now Henrietta understood Maurice's admonition.

She reached inside her pocket, opened the plastic bag one-handed, and groped for the baptism cap with her fingers.

She kept it folded in half, placed it tenderly behind his head, like a pillow, without moving one gossamer strand. She winced at the way it looked—his head resting against white satin, like the lining of a coffin.

"His name is Michael Patrick O'Toole," Lacey whispered.

"That's lovely," Henrietta said, pulling out the vial of holy water from her pocket.

Now, finally, came the familiar part, the part she used to worry about in front of a large congregation, that she might wake a sleeping baby into fear and rage when the droplets poured upon its forehead. This baby was silent as a stone.

"Michael Patrick O'Toole, I baptize you in the name of the Father, Son, and Holy Ghost." Henrietta's heart clenched at the word "ghost." She reached for Lacey's hand, and as she did so, she grasped the nurse's warm hand in her other hand. They formed a prayer circle around the baby in the smaller circle of his mother's arms.

"Let us say the *Our Father* together," Henrietta said.

Lacey's hands held their hands against the baby's now hard, still form. The three of them whispered the prayer together, only a few words in synchronicity. Our Father. Heaven. Give us. Deliver us. From Evil.

"Thank you," Lacey said. "And I know he is in Heaven, I know that! Now he is already up there. He went to sleep in my arms on this earth and the last thing he saw was my face. His own mother's face! And now he is waking up in Heaven—you know that too—and he will open his eyes to see the baby Jesus' face, right?"

She looked up at the nurse and then at Henrietta, waiting.

The nurse widened her eyes, but did not answer. She looked over to Henrietta for help.

"And at least he did not die alone," Henrietta said, remembering her mother's words.

"Oh, no. He was never alone. Not for one second since he's been here," Lacey declared. "Never, ever alone. And now he's in Heaven with all the other angels."

The nurse had turned down the lights. Lacey was a blurry figure in the darkened room. When she put her baby back into the incubator and leaned over him for one last kiss, Henrietta bowed her head again. There was no need for the formality of the prayers or litanies. Henrietta was relieved that it was over. A mother's kiss good-night and a favorite lullaby committed her son's soul to eternal rest.

The baby's body, Michael Patrick O'Toole's body, had been moved into the viewing room before Henrietta arrived. They must have needed that Neonatal bed right away. It was wrapped in a white plastic bag rather than the adult-sized black nylon one, and it had a front zipper halfway down its length, with clear plastic on the bottom half, like an upside-down dry cleaner's suit bag. Henrietta walked over to the gurney and unzipped the bag, carefully tucking it back down behind him and then pulling the white sheet up to his shoulders, like covers on a bed. She did not look at his face until the last moment.

One of the nurses had put his baptism cap upside down, affixed it with a hairpin, and Henrietta reached over to take it off, releasing the cotton candy–like swirl of saffron yellow hair. How could it be that hair, the dead part of all living things, always seemed so alive? She put the cap back in her pocket. Maurice had said that the mother was Catholic but not a word about the faith tradition of the father, so it would be better not to make assumptions. She glanced at the baby's face, now a solid blue-gray tone.

She walked over to flip the switch that turned on a green light above the outside of the closed door. She waited for the knock of the Patient Escort, using the time to locate the supplies she might need, pulling out the pink vomit basin, extra tissues, antibacterial wipes. She couldn't find a paper hospital gown to wear over her clothes, but her black sweater and pants would hide a multitude of possible stains.

When she opened the door, the first thing she noticed was the anxious expression on the face of the volunteer, a boy no older than thirteen, who stood on his toes trying to look over Henrietta's shoulder, wanting to look yet not wanting to see what might be waiting there. Behind him was a hospital security guard, holding the arm of a man who was handcuffed. The father did not seem much older than Lacey, definitely under twenty. Babies having babies.

"Coroner's case," the guard said, looking intently at Henrietta to make sure she understood.

Coroner's cases could have the bodies viewed but never touched by anyone other than hospital staff, or the evidence of the case would be considered tainted. The body was the most important evidence to prove or disprove that the person might have died under suspicious circumstances.

The father took one glimpse of his son's body and flung himself to the floor, bringing the security guard to his knees. He vomited at Henrietta's feet, soaking her shoes. Another thing she had forgotten to find in the supply closet—shoe covers. The relentless sound of violent retching continued, filling the room with a foul odor.

She stepped back and tried to wipe off her shoes. The stench was stronger now.

She took a small bottle of essence of tangerine aromatherapy oil out of her purse and placed a drop under each nostril to neutralize the smell, keep her from gagging.

The guard pulled the man up by his shirt collar and dragged him in the direction of the bathroom.

"For God's sake, clean your sorry ass up! You said you could handle this! Man up and face it, or I'm taking you back to County," the guard yelled.

Henrietta gasped. "Listen. You don't need to . . ."

"Don't need to what?" The guard blinked at her. "Be so rough with him?"

"Yes—actually—he's just lost his son. You know . . ."

"Didn't they tell you how that baby ended up here? Didn't they?"

"Well, no, but I don't see how that matters," she sputtered. "The baby's dead—that's all I think th it we need to know. There are medical confidentiality rights."

The guard stared at her.

"Shaken baby," he said. "That trumps the privacy rights of that bastard in there, don't you think?"

Henrietta reeled back as if he had slapped her face.

"I can't believe this. I saw that baby up on the unit and saw all those photos. And I just presumed he had some horrible illness."

"Not that his own daddy shook his brains loose and threw him against a concrete wall to shut up his crying."

"Jesus . . ."

"No offense, Ma'am, but I don't think Jesus has had anything to do with all this down here. But I'll still pray he's got that baby in His arms right now."

The toilet flushed, and she looked at the door and saw the boy was standing up.

"Time's up, you sorry bastard."

He shuffled over to the gurney, his head down. Henrietta had not noticed the leg chains before this moment.

"I thought I could do it. But I can't. It's too much," he stammered. Then he squinted his eyes, peering at her nametag.

"Chaplain? Reverend? Can you help me?"

"I don't know that I can, actually," Henrietta said.

"You can pray for me, can't you? Forgive me, Reverend, forgive me and pray for me."

His eyes were bloodshot, a muddy brown color, his face unshaved, with wisps of light red fuzzy hair on his chin. He stood and waited for her response.

The boy and the guard bowed their heads.

They waited for her to begin. But she couldn't say a word. The guard peeked up at her.

"Every sorry soul deserves a prayer," he whispered.

The prisoner fell to his knees then, his head cradled in cuffed hands. He began to sob in huge gasps. On the back of his neck was a scrolling tattoo, Michael Patrick in blues and greens. Henrietta closed her eyes and remained silent. Then the guard knelt beside him.

"Dear Lord," the guard began. "Have mercy on this man, a sinner. And take your sweet baby boy back home, where he will have no more pain, no more suffering. We thank you for his brief time with us. We failed to love him as your Son showed us how to love. Please forgive us as we try to forgive each other. Amen."

The prayer was exactly right. Henrietta kept her Book of Worship closed in her hands, and she was the only one in the room not on her knees. God would have to forgive her as well, for not being able to pray at a murderer's request.

The boy kept his head down even as the guard lifted him to his feet. Not another word was said, but Henrietta knew something had changed. Even the air in the room felt different.

Henrietta flipped the status light switch back to red after they left. It would be her duty to escort the body down to the morgue. She checked her watch. It had been forty-five minutes since she arrived for her shift. She would finish the case in under an hour.

She went over to the baby's body, forcing one last look. Against the white of the sheet, his skin was now an awful shade of gray, and her stomach lurched. What a terrible thing for any parent to see, no matter the circumstances.

Her own mother had been spared a viewing of her son's body after his accident. But she did see something that would always be associated with his violent death. It was the bloody shirt of the man who drove the car that killed him, the man who had been holding him during his last moments alive. Her mother had recognized her son's dark red silhouette from across the police station's waiting room. She had run toward the man, hands outstretched to trace the shape of her son's head with the tips of her fingers, softly and slowly. Then she had yanked her hands away, as if burned, when the human map beneath them trembled and heaved into sobs.

"I'm so, so sorry," the accidental killer cried out. "Is there anything I can do?"

"Give me your shirt," her mother said.

He took it off and handed it to her. And then their mother held him, naked from the waist in her arms, rocking him, like a baby, absolving him with her embrace.

Henrietta walked over to the supply cabinet and took the small scissors out of the drawer. She snipped a large lock of the sunshine hair, Lacey's son's hair, and put it in her pocket, wrapping the baptism cap carefully around it. She would find Lacey's address from the patient roster and send it to her with the baptism certificate.

She sealed the bag, being very careful not to let the zipper scratch his skin. Then she swaddled him in the blanket that was resting at the foot of the bed and carried him like this all the way to the morgue. She would tell his mother that her little boy had not made his last trip alone.

The Viewing Room MAY

The entrance doors to the hospital's viewing room do not carry warning signs for those about to bear witness to the unbearable. There is no preparation for the sight of the freshly dead body of a loved one last seen alive. All other senses fade into the background of the present moment, may even disappear from memory altogether. They might forget the salty taste of blood, after biting the knuckles of their hands smashed against mouths shocked open. They might forget the way death smells from the chemical postmortem wash, or the way death feels from the morgue's frozen drawer. But they will never forget the way death looks.

Chaplains must accompany all visitors, whether requested or not, as a nonnegotiable condition of access to this room. They carry books of sacred words to say out loud, as if anybody cares to hear another voice once the beloved's voice is forever silenced. All sounds—cries and sighs, wails and whimpers, and chants and curses—float weightless and powerless in this universe, this alien landscape without gravity. People entering this room are instantly and significantly disabled, helpless to make any sense of their surroundings because all senses except sight are disconnected. And since sight is the least reliable way to gather accurate information, what happens here is almost always misunderstood, misremembered, and tragically mistaken for a greater truth.

People come into this room looking for a spiritual experience that will transcend the physical experience of viewing the dead. They come here not because they are unafraid of death but because they are so afraid of death that they hope seeing it up close will lessen their fears. But their eyes betray them every time. They have been taught that "seeing is believing," so their faith must depend almost exclusively upon their vision. But if they see nothing—if they fail to see any signs of life in the body that lies motionless, scentless, speechless, and breathless before them—then what next?

The question always hangs in the air like a thought balloon above the body. What next? This is why sight is so important, the sense we trust and value most despite its constant deceptions. Sight is the most anticipatory sense. What we see in the distance prepares us for what lies ahead. The unforeseen attack is always the one that destroys us. It is true that people will never see what they think they come into this room looking for—the right answers to the lives under final examination. Yet it is also true that each human being leaves this room having seen something never seen before, which unquestionably changes each one of them, forever.

[GHOST DANCE]

It was late on Sunday night, Mother's Day, a day that had already seemed endless, when Henrietta, the chaplain on call for the hospital, received an urgent page to come to the patient in Room 204, who had requested spiritual support. Birdie, an elderly Pima Indian woman in the end stages of diabetic kidney failure, took up both of the room's hospital beds. With her own four hundred plus pounds and all the dialysis equipment, she needed a double room all to herself. The sole surviving member of her family, she had been airlifted from her reservation in Arizona in hopes of receiving a kidney transplant. Once she'd arrived, her condition had steadily deteriorated, disqualifying her as an eligible organ recipient. She would never be medically stable enough to be flown back home to die.

So she had received no outside visitors and soon began treating the hospital staff as if they were there for the sole purpose of keeping her entertained, like a twenty-four-hour revolving-door slumber party. She was a delightful storyteller and compassionate listener, but only a stalwart few managed to stay in her room for longer than a few minutes. Birdie was dying a slow and painful death, and the smell of her rotting body had become unbearable.

Henrietta put two drops of citrus aromatherapy oil underneath each nostril and rubbed more into her palms before she walked in. She rested her hand on Birdie's shoulder and glanced at her face. The jaundice from the failing liver had mixed with the dark magenta undertones of her skin, giving it a purple sheen. Her sightless eyes were open wide, staring straight ahead, the opaque irises and pupils spilling into the yellow-whites. Birdie's pupils, unable to take in any light, somehow managed to reflect light outward, flashing in strobe-like blinks. In the dark of the room, the rest of her body also glowed, wide and flat, wrapped in white gauze, splayed on the jumbo-sized metal serving tray of the two linked gurneys. She put her hands, webbed by the bandages into oversized paws, over her face when Henrietta touched her.

"I'm sorry, Birdie, did I wake you up?"

Henrietta noticed that Birdie's eyeglasses were on the side table. Hope in solid form, or "wearing the prayer," as Maurice, another chaplain and Henrietta's new best friend, often said. She had been visiting Birdie soon after Birdie had gone blind, trying to provide comfort, when Maurice came in with the eyeglasses and plopped them right on her face, without a word of warning. Hadn't he learned about announcing oneself before approaching blind patients? But as always, Maurice was the true visionary. The weight of those glasses on her nose transformed Birdie's face with an expression of absolute rapture, like someone under a hypnotic trance.

"I just had the most wonderful dream, Henny! And I was standing on my tiptoes again, looking up at a tall, handsome man. That was the best part," Birdie said.

"Tell me more," Henrietta responded, her holy trinity of words, never failing to air out even the most stifling of conversations. "Tell me more about your dream, sweetie," she whispered.

"Well, you'll love this one, Henny-girl. Big old me was wearing a size-four dress and high-heeled red shoes, and we were ghost dancing. Don't recall his face, but I could see his hands, big and strong. I could see his hands close around my waist, which in my dream, by the way, was so itty-bitty that his fingers could touch together at my back, and his thumbs touch together at my front. Now can you just imagine that?"

"It sounds lovely, Birdie."

"Oh, it was! Now you can tell that Chaplain Maurice he doesn't have to find me those red dancing shoes anymore but they already came up in my dream, right? Ask and you shall receive, right?"

Henrietta had been visiting Birdie for three months now, always on Sunday afternoons while still dressed in her church clothes and kitten-heeled pumps, so Birdie usually heard her coming down the hallway. But today she had stayed home from church and was wearing soft-soled moccasins. Birdie had told her how much she missed wearing pretty shoes, ever since her toes had been amputated. The gangrene wounds in her feet refused to heal. Henrietta glanced at Birdie's huge mummylike legs. The flesh-eating infection was moving quickly, but it had a lot of territory to cover. She could measure Birdie's prognosis by where the dry bandages ended and the weeping pus-filled ones began, like a moving demarcation line. It was now at the very top of her thighs, within inches of her femoral artery. It would not be much longer now.

"Birdie?" She stared at Birdie's chest and held her breath waiting for it to move. "Birdie?" she called out louder, her voice shaking with panic.

"Here. I'm still here," Birdie answered finally, and Henrietta closed her eyes in a silent prayer of thanks.

"You know, Henny-girl, I was thinking the silliest thing about you and me. How it's almost like we got our names switched way back when. Here I am, the one who looks more like a big-assed, clucking mother hen, and here you are, that Maurice has told me all about you, as tiny and light as a sparrow's feather. I guess you should have the name Birdie . . ."

"I'd been meaning to ask where you got . . ."

"Real name is Bird Chaser. Won't trouble you with the Indian word."

"Bird Chaser?"

"Oh, yes. And I grew my way into that name, for sure, I'm telling you true! I got a job for the Park Service in the canyon. Me running around, flapping and clapping my hands, and you better believe I chased those condors away from tourists and a few tourists away from the condors just so they wouldn't start trusting us idiots. Just leads to stupid killing. Not the condors, God knows, they don't kill."

"I've never seen a condor, but I'm sure they're beautiful."

Birdie laughed. "Oh, no, Henny, I know you haven't seen one, because they are sure not beautiful! They're just as ugly and fat and slumped over as I am! Big turkey vultures, lazy old things, who wait for the other, quicker birds like eagles to do the killing, and then wait and eat the leftovers."

Henrietta's stomach lurched. This conversation was not going in a positive direction, and she just could not handle talking about death. Even if it was her job to talk about whatever the patient wanted. Please not tonight. Not when she missed her own mother so much.

"I didn't hear you spray when you first came in, " Birdie said. "Go catch yourself a fresh breeze."

Henrietta walked over to the window and surveyed the collection of stuffed toy birds lined up on the ledge, each perched in front of a canister of room deodorizer. Birdie called it her "show and smell" display. It was a rite of passage for all who entered her contaminated space to choose one and spray it. The ritual had little or no practical effect. The spray did not touch the odor from Birdie's body. The only thing that helped at all were the discreetly placed trays of cat litter under her bed, which were changed every few hours with her colostomy bag.

The room freshener collection kept growing, but not as fast as Birdie's disease, which affected over half of the members of her tribe. Both her parents and older brothers and sisters had died of diabetes, all wheelchair bound at the end. Birdie never had breathing space between their deaths to fall in love and start her own family. Henrietta had already grown to love her as a surrogate mother. Birdie's warm spirit melted all professional boundaries away.

Henrietta reached for her favorite and sprayed it above her head, deeply inhaling the lushness of Tangerine Tango. She closed her eyes, pretending she had wandered into a tropical garden. For a few seconds, there was blessed relief from air that was worse than anything she had ever encountered in her months of chaplaincy, in the viewing room, in the emergency room, even in the morgue during an autopsy. She had learned this much. It was not the smell of death that was unbearable, but the smell of life spoiling away. She sprayed again and twirled in the fresh mist, dreaming of Birdie's dancing partner spinning her.

"Better, now?" Birdie asked. "Can you stand to stay with me for a while?"

"Of course, sweetie. It's not that bad."

"Not that bad? Really? Don't lie to me, Hen. This old carcass of mine hasn't seen the inside of a shower or tub in over two years. Mother Earth Spirit knows that even the sponges shrivel up and die when they come near me. But you know the worst part?"

"What is the worst part?" Henrietta asked, as she walked over to the bedside.

She cleared the visitor chair of two baskets, woven by Birdie's mother long ago and filled with medicine bundles. These were the only personal possessions Birdie had been allowed to bring with her because her weight had strained the helicopter's maximum load. The baskets were placed there so that Birdie could hear them being moved and be forewarned that someone had taken a seat. She smiled at the way Birdie started all her visits. Worst part/best part questions framed their pastoral conversations—and Henrietta was always eager to see how Birdie could come up with anything that qualified for best, as she lay there dying, rotting from the outside in.

"Here it is, then," Birdie said. "The worst part about being a sick, fat, smelly old woman that chases everybody away with her stink. The worst part is just being stuck inside of me. Where is a real out-of-body experience when you most need it?" Birdie sighed. "But the best part is that I don't have any more nightmares. In my dreams, I am always dancing." Birdie closed her eyes again, as if she could transport herself back into her party shoes by shutting the lids.

Henrietta was sure she had fallen asleep again, and not wanting to wake her from her dream, she started to get up from the chair.

"You remember what to do, right? When my time comes?" Birdie's eyes were open again, her lips tight, chin trembling.

"Yes, Birdie. I remember." Henrietta reached over and held Birdie's bandaged hand in hers.

Birdie had put the Spiritual Care office on alert that when she died she needed sage burned because the scent of sage, of the open prairies of her native lands, would carry her spirit back home. Henrietta had found sage incense sticks and left them in Birdie's bedside drawer. She could not light them, of course, or the smoke alarms would go off, but Birdie had said her soul would be so eager to leave, so quick to find an escape, that it would take only the spark of rubbing the sticks together.

"Don't worry, Birdie," Henrietta said. "I have everything ready . . . I mean . . ." She stammered, not wanting to sound as if she was rushing her out of the world.

"Oh, Henny, that's good, because I'm ready too! I've been getting ready for this for ages now. They don't call it morbid obesity for nothing! But I'm not scared, Hen. I want you to know that. And I'm not just saying that. Death doesn't scare me. It's been my shadow my whole life. You know how most people know they are going to die but don't really believe it? Not until it's right up front in their face?"

"Yes," Henrietta said.

It was true that people did not want to think about death, but she also believed that they did not have to think about how they were going to die. They simply had to think about how they wanted to live. Then the trick was to live that way up until the last moment, when they had to stop. She had seen fourteen patients die since she had become the on-call overnight weekend chaplain six weeks ago. And she remembered every one of them, exactly how they looked the moment life left their bodies and how they looked afterward. There was no such thing as resting in peace when it came to death. The peace had to be found in life or not at all. And somehow, Birdie had managed to find that kind of peace and spread it around her, sweetening every bit of space she occupied.

"I admire the way you are leaving us, Birdie. My mother always said that a lady should not be remembered for the grandness of her entrances, but for the gracefulness of her exits."

Birdie laughed. "Oh, I sure do love hearing about that mama of yours!" She scooped Henrietta's hand into both of hers.

"Tell me what color this week? Red or pink?"

Henrietta held the fingernails of her other hand up to the light coming from the window, not wanting to take away the one that Birdie was holding. They played this guessing game about the name of her nail polish. Last week was Cotton Candy Swirl and the week before was Strawberry Cream Dream. At first, she was embarrassed that so many colors had such vivid food associations. Birdie was on a feeding tube and had not tasted a meal in over a year. But she soon discovered that Birdie was delighted to talk about food, smell food, and even found a way to taste it, when the nurses would bring in different flavored lip balms for her. The scent of Café-au-Lait never failed to pick up her spirits, no matter the time of day or night.

"Pink again," Henrietta said.

"But what kind of pink? Tell me the name of it! C'mon, tell me . . ."

Henrietta examined her nails, trying to remember. The color was very pale pink, with a metallic sheen and a touch of gold sparkles. Pink Champagne Bubbles? No, that was not it. Something to do with evening dreams.

"Sunset Reverie," she blurted out, finally remembering.

"Oh, yes!" Birdie exclaimed. "That's perfect."

"Yes," Henrietta said. She sighed again, and it surprised them both when it came out like a moan.

"You are sad tonight, dearie. What is it?"

Henrietta was ashamed and hesitated to tell her the truth. Here she was, the comforter needing comforting. But she never lied to Birdie.

"Oh, you know. I'm sorry. It's the Mother's Day thing."

She did not need to say more, because they had both lost their mothers years ago.

"Oh, Henny—that reminds me! I just got a special Mother's Day treat for you! It's called French Vanilla, although what's French about it, I have no idea, unless it just smells fattening and rich, like something wonderful and buttery baking in the oven. Go bring me over a whiff of that! It may even cheer us both up."

Henrietta went over to the windowsill again, found the air freshener, and sprayed it around Birdie's bed.

"The Pet Therapy trainer brought me that," Birdie said. "And you know one thing for sure—she's the expert around here on how to get rid of nasty odors fast."

Henrietta laughed, the vanilla scent filling her with sudden joy. She was touched that Birdie had remembered that this was her favorite childhood memory, when her mother would bake her vanilla custards on snow days back in Maine. But then Birdie remembered every person's story and always found a way to give it back later, wrapped in her own kind of motherly love.

"But those dogs are so well groomed!" Henrietta said. Her favorite was Her Majesty, the Great White Pyrenees, with her gleaming silky white coat. She was as large as a miniature horse but so light on her feet that she floated down the hospital corridors like a cloud. "Not Her Majesty? She smells like a rain shower!"

"No, it's that sweet old Golden Retriever. Not his fault, but he is starting to lose control of his bowels," Birdie said. "Apparently that's a real problem on these elevators, worse than a fart in a sweat lodge . . . I don't need to tell you! The poor old thing is too arthritic to go up the stairs. I do love that dog. He sparks me. You know the one I mean?"

"Mr. Right."

Everyone knew his name. The pet therapist who owned him had been married and divorced five times. She had given up on the male species of the human population.

"That's his name, you bet it is! Mr. Right has made a promise to me . . . to save a spot next to him in Heaven if he gets there first. It's a race too close to call, because I can smell his body going to seed as fast as mine. You know the best part about him?"

Henrietta shook her head and then remembered that Birdie could not see her. "No, tell me the best part, sweetie."

"Quite simple really. Mr. Right is the first male I ever met that doesn't care that I smell so bad. As a matter of fact that only makes him love me more, don't you think?"

"Yes. But the truth is that everyone here loves you, Birdie."

And this truth was in plain view. The windowsill was overflowing with gifts, each staff member who had met her trying to figure out a way to stay in the room without gagging. Birdie welcomed every one of them, no matter what each one had to do to her—awful things: scraping off dead flesh, changing burning catheters, pushing and pulling folds of her skin back and forth to expose the bedsores to the air. And yet she appeared grateful for each and every person who came into her room, thanking them for their care, and remembered each name, each person's family, each person's story. She was the un-official chaplain in this hospital, Maurice had often told her.

"Yes, you hospital people are my family now. Still, nobody loves us the way our mamas love us, right? Mama's here now. Right here with us. Don't you see her? Standing right next to you?"

Henrietta was worried again. She had never heard Birdie talk like this before. Whose mother did Birdie think was in the room with them? She was afraid to ask. If Birdie saw her own mother, that would mean she was dying for sure, and if she was seeing Henri-etta's mother, someone she had never met, then her mind was going, and the rest would quickly follow.

"I'm not sure I understand, Birdie. You can feel another presence here, like a ghost?"

"Sure can! Ghost, angel, whatever you want to call it. She's been here all day. That's why I had the nurse page you. I wanted you to meet her."

Henrietta started to look around the room. She did not believe in ghosts, but she did believe in Birdie's ability to see with the eyes of the spirit.

"But how do you know someone else is here now if you can't see anything?"

As soon as she said this, Henrietta wished she could suck the words out of the air back into her throat, or spray something on them to make them sound less harsh, less judgmental. She knew better than to argue a patient out of her delusion, particularly one that was giving her so much pleasure. Birdie did not say a word. Had Henrietta ruined her dream?

"Listen to me, now," Birdie interrupted, turning her face back toward Henrietta, her blind eyes neon yellow lasers, roving the room, searching for a target. "You don't have to be sorry. But I want you to know that I don't have to see her to know she is here. And you understand it better than anybody else in this hospital."

"I'm sorry, Birdie. I know that God's presence can't be seen, but I thought you were talking about people." Dead people, she wanted to add, but held back.

"Yes, but my people believe that spirits are like the wind, or maybe they are part of the wind, and we can only see the change the wind makes in the trees, and feel and smell the difference in the air when it moves."

As soon as Birdie said this, Henrietta felt the air thickening and settling in around them. Then she felt a gentle pressure at the back of her neck, and around her shoulders, as if layers of warming blankets were being wrapped around her.

"You see?" Birdie said.

"Yes," Henrietta said. "I see."

The wheels at the bottom of the beds began to squeak. Birdie's whole body was shaking.

"Are you feeling all right, Birdie? Are you in any pain?"

"No pain!" she exclaimed. "And better than all right. Better! This old body hasn't felt this good in so many years, but I can't wait to let it go. I told that organ donation guy yesterday . . . that if anybody wants any piece of it . . . well, then, they are welcome to it! Leave it out on those canyons and have those condors give me a big send-off! Sky burial."

"Or maybe, you don't have to have a body at all, Birdie." Henrietta wanted to fly with her now. "You will be weightless, like air."

"I like that, Henny-girl, I do!"

Birdie sank deep into the mattress. Her eyes were closed and she began to hum to herself. Then she stopped and raised her head slightly, turning toward Henrietta.

"Hey there. You want to know what I've been thinking about? I've been thinking about what Heaven smells like!"

"Really? And what do you think it smells like?"

"Why nothing at all! That's what I think," Birdie said, laughing. She had clearly given this a lot of thought. "It will be like God's breath. That's what keeps me going down here . . . to think that every piece the docs take off of me just brings me closer and closer to being no body at all . . . so I can fly so lightly into that place where I will not smell bad ever again."

"Yes, I believe that, too, Birdie. That's lovely."

Birdie sat up suddenly again, looking straight ahead, holding her arms outstretched.

"Yes, I will!" Birdie shouted to the empty air. "Yes, I am going to be right there."

Henrietta rushed over to calm her, tried to embrace her, but Birdie was so large that Henrietta could not hold her or keep her from thrashing. Birdie's body was convulsing now, and she snapped her head back and forth and opened her eyes wide, now glistening an iridescent pale green. She shook so violently that the litter boxes beneath the beds rustled, making muffled, scurrying sounds.

An alarm screeched. It was Birdie's heart monitor. The nurse who had paged Henrietta rushed into the room and shut the machine off. She did not call a code because they all knew that Birdie was DNR.

And just like that, Birdie was gone. Henrietta felt as if she were suddenly caught in a cold draft of air and would never be warm again, the invisible blankets yanked off her shoulders. For a moment, she was paralyzed with shock and grief and could not think of what she should do next. But the nurse knew exactly what to do. She smoothed back Birdie's long hair from her face and removed each tube, one by one, from her still body.

Henrietta could not look at her any longer, but she had to keep her promise. She opened the drawer and rubbed the incense sticks together. She kept her eyes shut and felt a cool breeze as Birdie's final breath caught its sweet sage-scented ride home.

Birdie was never without visitors in the viewing room. For sixteen hours, staggered over all three hospital shifts, every staff member who had cared for her came in to see her one last time. And they lingered there, comforting one another, laughing and talking, not wanting the party to end. Birdie's enormous body had been completely bathed—the dialysis nursing unit's final gift to her. She smelled heavenly.

Where's an out-of-body experience when you really need one?

The last person to request a viewing was Maurice, who brought the Pet Therapy dog into the room with him. Mr. Right. Henrietta threw her arms around the dog's thick golden fur. He smelled like Maurice's cologne. She wasn't the first one to hug this dog today and certainly would not be the last. He was the kind of dog that Birdie used to say woke up with his tail wagging, thinking to himself, *Who gets to love me today?*

Maurice walked over to Birdie. He took something out of his forest-green, distressed-leather carrying case.

He unzipped Birdie's body bag, carefully and gently, peeling it back until her naked, mutilated feet were exposed. Then he placed two enormous white socks over them and then turned the socks around. There were bright red strappy sandals painted on them, and pretty, dainty feet, the skin rosy-toned, healthy, alive. And the *trompe l'oeil* toenails puffed up proudly, sparkly and shiny, dusted with a topcoat polish of pink and gold glitter. Sunset Reverie.

After Maurice left, the only sound in the viewing room was Mr. Right's heavy panting. He continued to sniff around Birdie's head as if he were looking for a different smell, the one that only he had loved. He began to whine softly and then pawed at Henrietta's leg, impatiently, as if he wanted something from her. A treat of some kind? But she didn't have anything to give him. She looked down at him, holding her empty hands out to him, but he kept jerking his head back and forth between her and Birdie. It reminded her of the old Lassie shows, when the dog was always trying to tell the parents that Timmy was in some kind of trouble, stuck in a well or dangling off a cliff, and they needed to go save him. Then she knew what he wanted. She lifted the old dog in her arms and laid him gently on the gurney, standing against him like a human guardrail so he wouldn't fall. She held his warm body there with hers and closed her eyes. She had a vision then that would give her peace every time she remembered Birdie. In her mind's eye, she saw two kindred souls gracefully exit the stage together, one four-legged and the other with arms as big and wide as wings, sharing one last dance.

The Viewing Room JUNE

There is no privacy in the viewing room. A video camera records everything. The film would make an unappealing reality show, given its steadfast refusal to change the scenery. And most of the moments in here are predictable and grimly mundane. But there are shocks—remarkable moments—not always tragic but nevertheless unforgettable. It is impossible to imagine these moments happening in any other place but this very room.

The dead may lose their voices, but their stories and often their most guarded secrets are still being told here. The naked corpse reveals not only the way one died but also a great deal more about the way one lived. Fathers stare at daughters whose private parts may be pierced in unfathomable places; sons gape at mothers with surgical scars from unknown operations; lovers gasp at the sudden sight of the body unsupported by the accustomed props such as spray-on tans, false teeth, and fake hairpieces. What remains of natural origin can be horrifying in its meagerness.

Do any of us ever see one another as we truly are? Would the dead want to be seen under such harsh, unforgiving lighting, particularly by the same people who think they know them best and would always love them regardless of past mistakes and hidden flaws in their design? The hospital never asks this question of patients when they are admitted—despite the inordinate amount of paperwork involved in getting sick, in getting hurt, in trying to heal, and finally in dying, despite the countless consent forms signed before death, giving permission to do unspeakable things to their persons.

If properly informed about the possible consequences, it is unlikely that anybody would consent to being laid out for this kind of scrutiny. The survivors make the decision to come into the viewing room under the most stressful, time-sensitive circumstances. They are reluctant to give up one more chance to see their beloved, even if they saw them alive only a few hours ago, in spite of the profound desire to remember them as healthy and full of spirit. They are more afraid of losing one last sweet image than they are of acquiring one new hideous one. It is a devil's choice many live to regret.

[HAVING WORDS]

"I'll take the ex-wife, and you take the girlfriend," Maurice whispered. "I have seniority and I get first pick. Whatever we do, we can't let them meet anywhere in this hospital and have words. Is that a deal?"

Henrietta didn't answer. She was staring at Maurice's salad bowl as he ladled out beets on top of his cottage cheese, instantly turning the top of his salad puffy and pink, like necrotic brain tissue. Her stomach lurched. She had not been able to hold down a full meal since fulfilling her Clinical Pastoral Care unit and its most dreaded final requirement, witnessing an autopsy. Now she could tell a patient's family, candidly, that she knew, slice by slice, how the procedure was handled, and could reassure them that the body was always treated with care and dignity. It was just bad luck, the morgue clinician had told her, shrugging his shoulders, that the case she had been called in to witness was a ten-year-old girl.

The girl's mother had found her early that morning. She had hung herself in her closet with a jump rope. She had left a note, presumed suicide, but because of the age it was a coroner's case and an autopsy was legally required. Nobody had warned Henrietta how autopsies began, with the face and the skin peeled off, starting right under the chin.

"How did you do it, Maurice?" she asked, keeping her voice low as they scuttled forward to the soup line. "How could you stand to see one?"

He shook his head.

"Never saw it. A person doesn't see what they are not looking at—didn't actually *see* anything. I put Vaseline over my contacts. Couldn't see a damn thing, thank God."

"Maurice? Really?"

"Sure. All the Spiritual Care Department manual requires is that a chaplain intern must be present in the morgue while an autopsy is being performed. And I was there. I was in the room. But I knew better than to focus on all the gory details."

"But that's the whole point of it, Maurice, we are supposed to know all the gory details . . ."

"Oh, my God, spare me the 'better-off-knowing' argument, all right? It's toxic knowledge, Hen. Useless. Ominous. Look at you, Exhibit A, just wasting away. Haunts you forever. It's like seeing the outside air temperature on the airplane map screen when you're forty thousand miles up—what good is that little scientific tidbit of information going to do for you, unless you plan to take a stroll out on the wing and need to know it is minus 150 degrees so you can dress warmly?"

Henrietta laughed. "It's just that I thought I had to see it in order to understand it."

"Oh, for God's sake, really? Tell me then, Miss Understand-It-All. What colorful visual memory of that poor little girl's insides did you see in there that helped you understand anything about why Patty died the way she did? Please, enlighten me. Please."

On the last "please," the tray in his hands shook so hard that his iced coffee fell over. He had a chronic familial tremor triggered by stress.

"Shit," he said. "I'll be right back."

When Henrietta took the tray from him, she saw that his eyes were filled with tears. And then it hit her. He knew that little girl's name.

By the time he came back, he had calmed down. He put the coffee, now covered with a double lid, on the tray, and took the ruined salad off and dumped it.

"Oh, Maurice. I had no idea. I'm so sorry. Patty was one of your patients?"

He sighed and shook his head silently. Then he put his arm around her shoulders and led her around to the other side, where the breads, cheeses, and lunch meats were kept in huge bins. He reached for the largest plastic bowl, bigger than the one he had filled before.

"Now, let's concentrate on putting lunch together. It may be hours before you have the chance to eat again."

"All right, I know." Henrietta took it from his hands. She would wait for a better time to talk about this. Maurice hated emotional scenes, particularly in the cafeteria. She held up the empty bowl. "If I fill this up and top it off with blue cheese dressing, will you at least tell me one more thing?"

Maurice took it from her and started to layer the bottom of her plate with croutons, mashing them down like piecrust. "Maybe. Go ahead, I'm listening."

Two of the Pet Therapy dog trainers, volunteers from the Westwood Humane Society, Sherry and Jo, were waving at them from the soup side, clearly within earshot. They adored Maurice because he gave them the most patient referrals. They were wearing matching red sweater-vests, home sewn by Sherry's mother, with tan felt dog-bone shapes glued all over them.

She moved closer to him and lowered her voice. "Why do you want the ex-wife?"

Maurice laughed. "So, you *were* listening!"

He looked relieved. He must have thought she had been going to ask a very different kind of question. "Oh, the ex-wives. They're always easier, relatively speaking, low-drama types. You know: wifely, with a blessedly simple agenda, just checking off an item on the after-death to-do list. Make sure he's really dead—check— and then they're out of there. But the second ones often still love the poor guy, so there is the usual—well, you know—messy stuff. And you are dressed more appropriately for that kind of thing than

I am today, anyway. We really need to do a closet purge, one of these days."

Henrietta gazed down at her clothes. Black slacks, mint green silk shirt, and dark brown jacket. All right, he had a point. She was a bit off on her color coordination. She looked like a rotting pea pod. But then what is the proper outfit for escorting a woman into the viewing room to see the freshly dead body of her boyfriend? Fashion had never interested her. She was the only one in her high school who was grateful to wear uniforms, to have the daily morning decision taken away. She often wondered if this was one of the reasons she wanted to be an ordained minister—the luxury of wearing robes. Usually she wore black. It always looked professional and did not show stains. But ever since she had lost one of her favorite patients, Birdie, a diabetic Pima Indian, she had started to wear green in her memory. Birdie had loved the color green, the color of hope, she had said. Oh, God, she missed that dear woman. She missed Birdie so much she had become a walking purpose ribbon. But what was wrong with that?

"Maurice, what do you mean that I'm dressed appropriately for a viewing?"

Maurice seemed to frown at her in the reflection of the sneeze guard, although the thick plastic barrier blurred his expression out. But she knew he was irritated because he put the tray down to use his hands. When she asked too many questions, he swatted the air at her, as if she were a noisy mosquito buzzing on the outside of his life.

"Well, it's all right, really. It's suitably tragic. Puke green top, brown jacket, black slacks—camouflage for the physical and emotional vomitorium you will inevitably become when you deal with the dead guy's girlfriend. She was the one who brought him in, so she will be a train wreck."

The woman in front of them in the cashier line turned completely around and put her finger to her lips, glaring at them. She was in scrubs, the ones with dancing giraffes. Familiar face. Pediatric Recovery.

"HIPAA," she hissed, as she took her finger away and shook her head. HIPAA was the federal law that protected medically confidential records. A reported violation of HIPAA, an employee saying any personal information about a patient in a public area, could cost them their jobs.

Maurice smiled at her. "Oh, my goodness, I forgot to use my indoor voice."

They went over to their usual table by the window and put her sweater and purse on the remaining chairs so they would not be overheard. She sat down. When Maurice started to take his food off his tray, she stopped him and slid the tray over to the side. Then she reached over for his hands. He bowed his head, assuming that she was about to say grace.

"No, I don't want to pray with you, Maurice. I don't want to talk to God. I want to talk to you. Just tell me what's been going on. Please."

He had been distant with her the last few weeks. This was the first time they had managed to have a meal together in over a month, and only because their shifts, her night shift and his day shift, had overlapped this morning and they had to share this assignment. Henrietta loosened her grip but did not completely let go of his hands. She looked into his eyes and noticed that they were bloodshot, as if he had been up all night crying, and the right eyelid was twitching. She did not want to cause him any more stress, but she wanted to understand.

"Listen, I know you have been avoiding me lately. Are you OK? Have I done anything to upset you?"

He shook his head and gave her hands a quick squeeze before letting go. Then he tapped at the window. Sherry and Jo's dogs were outside in the courtyard. Bitsy and Teensie, two identical Great Danes, lifted their enormous heads, looked around, and then settled back into sleep. They never barked and their movements were slow and deliberate, as they had been trained never to make a sudden movement that might scare the patient. Maurice's dog, a Border Collie mix, had failed Pet Therapy training. He once tore the face off a pediatric oncology ward patient's teddy bear. Maurice now called him his "Borderline" Collie. Maurice leaned his head against the glass, gazing at the dogs, and did not say anything for several minutes. This alarmed Henrietta more than the fatigue in his eyes. Maurice always kept the conversation moving, rescued her from sinking into dark spells of too much introspection.

"I do have a confession to make to you," he said finally, turning to look at her. "And I would like to ask your forgiveness."

"My forgiveness?" Henrietta was stunned. "What in the world can you possibly have done that would need my forgiveness?"

"Sins of omission, not commission, my dear." His shoulders sagged, and he lowered his head again for a moment. When he looked back up at her, his chin trembled. "It's not about what I have done, but what I haven't done. I should have told you about Patty weeks ago, right away, and I didn't. And I am truly sorry for that." He sounded so formal, so serious, as if he were officiating a memorial service.

"Tell me now, sweetie."

"Well, to begin with, I did know her. But not as a patient here."

He paused. Maurice had many lives outside the hospital. He was an actor at the West Hollywood Improv Center. A flamenco dance instructor. He was also a passionate gay rights activist, speaking at schools throughout Los Angeles about tolerance. Did he meet Patty at her school? But Henrietta knew that she must not ask any more questions, that she must wait for him to tell her in his own time, in his own way.

He sighed. "And here you are, unable to eat anything for months, and it should have been me down there, with Patty, bearing witness. I should have seen it through to the bitter end."

He was openly crying now. He took his napkin and held it against his eyes.

"Why didn't you tell me?"

She was ashamed to hear the squeaky note of hurt in her voice, as if the worst thing about a ten-year-old girl's suicide was that her friend did not rush to confide in her.

"I was being selfish," he said. "I tried to keep it my own little pocket-sized tragedy and carry it around with me before I showed it to anybody."

He pulled out a bright pink envelope from his inside jacket pocket. He handed it to her. "Please don't read it out loud," he said.

Henrietta opened the envelope and took out a folded piece of paper, the same hot pink as the envelope, but with a border of pink butterflies.

Dear Mom and Dad,
I told you school was too hard.
I can't go back.

Henrietta stared at the words and then closed her eyes. That small, pale face held so much pain inside, long before the forensic scalpel touched it.

He took the paper back from her. "The parents never saw this. I couldn't bear to show it to them. The paramedics who were called to the house found it and gave it to the ER nurse. I spared them seeing these last words. At least I managed that."

"Oh, God, Maurice. I am so sorry. How awful."

"Yes, awful. But I am the one who's sorry. I am the most sorry-ass person here because I was the one who encouraged Patty to go back to school, to stand up to the bullies. I told her parents that she was ready to go back."

Patty had been a hotline caller at the twenty-four-hour crisis line Maurice answered at the Gay and Lesbian Center.

"She was being beaten up at school. She got a crush on one of those mean popular girls. They were brutal and then . . ." He stopped at the sound of the on-call pager beeping. "Oh, here we go—perfect timing!"

Then he pulled it out of his pocket again, turned off the sound, and left it pulsating on the table between them, without glancing at it, treating it like a prematurely delivered restaurant bill he had no intention of claiming. Liberated from its silk-lined trap, the pager scuttled across the table like a crab, a few inches with each vibration, and she had to catch it before it fell off her side. And they say machines don't have minds of their own.

She couldn't avoid reading the text message. *ER calling.* That meant lunch was officially over because *ER calling* was the cue that the body was ready to be viewed. She picked up the pager and scrolled through the rest of the information. The girlfriend had brought him in, dead on arrival.

"Time's up," she said, leaning over to hug Maurice good-bye.

One body, two viewings. One viewing room, two chaplains. They would have to coordinate their entries and exits very carefully. She looked at the huge salad she had not touched and shrugged her shoulders.

"Talk about an instant appetite suppressant."

"Tell me about it. Only perk of this job." Maurice sighed and cleared the tray. "Didn't I tell you that I used to weigh four hundred pounds before I started working here?"

"Really? There's a lot I don't know about your former life," Henrietta said, laughing.

"That's for sure," he said raising his eyebrows at her, and then looking down at the beeping pager, winced. "OK, here's the deal. The ex is coming in from Bakersfield at one for the viewing." He looked at his watch. "Legally she has no right to see him, but since she is already on her way, I'm going to try to get her in and out of there in a heartbeat—so to speak. OK, then, you can have as much time as you need with the girlfriend. Stay in a holding pattern with her up in the chapel, and wait there for me to page you with an all-clear."

"Sounds like a plan."

"Good. I'll use the South Wing Surgery elevators so we don't run into one another. We want to avoid some kind of tacky catfight, just to be safe."

"You got it," she said. She reached out and put her hand against his cheek. "But remember, Maurice," she whispered, as other people were gathering at the elevator, "we aren't finished talking about this, right?"

He gave her a sad smile and then turned around to wait for the elevator.

She walked back into the Spiritual Care office to sign in and to retrieve her supplies. She had learned to bring in her own and not depend on the hospital to refill the viewing room cabinets. She peered into the black canvas bag to make sure they were all there. The tissues, aromatherapy bottle, extra set of paper scrubs, and latex gloves were layered on top of boxes of miniature Bibles.

She looked at the referral form she had picked up in the office. Decedent's faith tradition was not listed. Not that it necessarily mattered anymore. The girlfriend might not share his religion. "Minister to the living, not the dead," the manual stated. Sometimes she thought that people in the viewing room held on to the belief that saying the right words would work like a blessed abracadabra to open the doors of Heaven. Henrietta had learned that there are no right words in the viewing room. Words had no substance in there; they were free-floating, meaningless. The viewing room was a place designated for seeing, not hearing. Of course, she would say a prayer when specifically asked to do so. She had finally learned to do that after the first disaster with the teenage baby killer. Yet she found that even the loveliest words, the Lord's Prayer or the Twenty-third Psalm, were swallowed up in the stale air of that windowless space. She had found it more healing to say as little as possible.

The elevator doors to the Emergency waiting area opened, and Henrietta spotted her right away. People in shock could be recognized from a distance. They unconsciously assumed a defensive posture, hunched over, as close to a fetal position as one could manage while still standing, stuck in vertical crash-landing position. The first thing Henrietta tried to do with a family member in shock was to get down to their level and talk with them there. It was another reason to wear dark slacks.

"I am so sorry," Henrietta said, kneeling down beside her.

When the woman realized that Henrietta was talking to her, she stood up straight. "Excuse me, please," the woman said, her voice husky, as if she had been crying. She had a bandage and a patch over one eye. "I've got to finish this phone call. It's private. Do you mind giving me some room here?"

The woman had not been crouching down in shock. She had been leaning next to the low-slung bank of windows, trying to get the best cell reception. And she was not waiting for an escort to the viewing room but trying to call her husband to pick her up, since she had crashed her car.

Henrietta decided to go down to the viewing room and see if she could find the girlfriend there. She went inside and found Maurice in the bathroom, scrubbing his hands. The water in the sink was pale green. "Help me get this stuff off," he said to her. "I feel like I've been slimed."

"What happened to you?"

"You won't believe this. I still can't believe it happened so fast. I thought I would give her a moment of privacy. I didn't leave the room—you know, I can't—but I turned my back on her for half a minute and that's all it took. I turned around and she had a marker and was writing all over him! So I wrestled the damn marker out of her hand, but two seconds later, she's got another one! She'd brought in a whole bag of them with her! God, these gigantic handbags you women carry, a person could hide a baby elephant in them."

"Oh, my God. What words?"

Maurice shuddered, closing his eyes. "Trust me. You don't want to know."

"I'm dying to know, actually, and you're dying to tell me."

Maurice shrugged his shoulders. "Well, all right. I guess I deserve that after telling you the ex would be easy. She yanked the plastic body bag off of him and wrote across his stomach, I WAS HERE FIRST, and then put a big green arrow pointing down."

"No way!"

"Oh, yes. That arrow was pointing one way. Could see it from a 747 jumbo jet. Permanent marker, by the way, as you can see. All I could do was cover him back up. Then I paged the morgue to pick him up and escorted her out the front door."

"But what about the girlfriend?"

"Well, that was a huge charting mistake. It was actually a boyfriend. And he bolted as soon he saw what was going on. I still have a few ice skating moves left in me. The moment I saw his head pop in the door, I whirled him out of there so fast, the ex-wife never saw him."

"He's gone then? No second viewing?"

"You think we needed any more drama in there? Believe me, I've had enough of the Hell Hath No Fury scenes. Is this karmic justice or what? For making fun of your green wardrobe? It's not just the color of hope, honey."

"Seriously? An arrow pointing to his penis? She was still that attached? Like she was planting a flag or something?"

Maurice looked at her. "Well, it can be quite hard to let go of these things," he said, laughing.

"I guess, if you say so . . ."

Maurice grew serious. "I felt sorry for her, actually. God knows it's not easy for any of us to sort out our feelings. I thought about it once. Came close to doing it, thinking if I liked men so much, maybe I needed to be a woman."

"Really? You never told me that."

"Oh, yes. I tried a lot of treatments, back then. I joined one of those religious groups that promised to 'pray the gay away.' That didn't do it. Then I tried reparation therapy, paid psychologists who tried to convince me that I was broken and needed to be repaired—thank God California has banned those awful people. How many Pattys do we need before we figure out what harm we do? Oh, and finally, I went to a transgender specialist. The ultimate fix. Couldn't go through with the surgery. Just couldn't do that to a body that had been so good to me, had always been a joy to me."

"I had no idea, Maurice. I had no idea how much you must have been hurting."

"Well, thank you for that. Very few people have any idea. The worst pain is hiding who you really are, betraying yourself and everyone else with the lies. That's why I can't really blame her for trying to have the last word."

"Literally," Henrietta said.

And for the first time, laughter filled the viewing room.

The Viewing Room JULY

People rarely close their eyes or even blink when they are in the viewing
room, as if the intensity of their stares will make the body move. Their secret fantasy is that the body will rise up and start to walk and talk and get
back to ordinary business, like Lazarus. The trouble with all those Bible stories is not necessarily that people take them seriously and literally, but that
they don't read the follow-up studies.

Research shows that many of these characters existed in real life. A guy
named Lazarus lived at the time of Jesus, was probably a close friend, but
certainly was not a person to be envied, at least not after the miracle. Poor
old Lazarus was a wanted man with a spiritual bounty on his head. Immediately after he was revived, his tomb shrouds sticking like bandages to
putrefying flesh, he was on the run. Jews and Gentiles alike were frantic to
hunt him down as a body of evidence to prove or disprove their particular
beliefs.

The sight of a dead man raised from the grave changes everything. The
glorious reflected light of a second birth must break all barriers of time and
space. For all who were blessed to be in its presence, that light would
stick forever on the insides of their eyelids and make them see everything
and every person, from that moment onward, clearer and lovelier than ever
before. Moving forward guided by this light, they would never again be

afraid of death. Then they would understand that the profound mystery of life is not that it ends, but that it ever begins. The rest of their lives would be one sweet, deep exhalation of relief.

It is no wonder that the desperate search for another Lazarus has continued for over two thousand years. People come into the viewing room hoping to witness a miracle that will engender a fresh new set of beliefs. But miracles need the movement of light and air and have no prayer of bursting forth in this windowless room. There will never be a spectacular entrance or exit of the spirit in a sparkling flash. The dead do not come back to life in the viewing room and bring important messages to the ones left behind. Yet the living are changed forever by what they see here. Or by what they fail to see.

[STAGGERED DEPARTURES]

The call came the way Anna's mother had predicted, through a stranger's voice. Still, she wasn't prepared for the news-anchor quality of this woman's tone, trained to deliver messages of personal tragedy.

"Yes, I'm Anna Green."

"Then Melanie Green is your mother?"

"Yes."

"Ms. Green, I'm a social worker at UCLA Medical Center. I'm so sorry to tell you this. Your mother was found unconscious at the Rescue Mission and brought here by ambulance. She is . . . well, she . . ." The voice cracked and started to shatter into sharp, icy fragments that chopped the sentence she was trying to speak.

"Is my mother dead?" Anna pressed the phone tightly to her ear so she could hear every word. It made her head throb. Nothing was said. Why was it such a hard question to answer? Either she was dead, or she wasn't. "Please. Just tell me!"

Again the roaring, thundering silence. Anna heard a muffled conversation as the social worker covered the phone with her hand. Her professionally flatlined voice soon returned.

"No, she's not dead. But only the attending doctor can give you any details. I can tell you, however, that she has deteriorated over the last twenty-four hours. I'm so sorry."

Anna could feel her throat tightening, but she refused to cry, saying, "I'm six hours away by plane. Adding time to get back and forth from airports, it could take as long as eight hours before I arrive."

Anna wanted to seal herself into a closed envelope of time, to be insulated from a full-out panic attack. "I'll tell the nurses," the social worker answered, accompanied by the clicking of keys on a computer. "I understand you're the next of kin and your mom designated you as the decision maker. When you arrive, you can talk with the doctors about keeping with her wishes."

Anna wanted to scream into the phone that nothing about her mother's death was in keeping with anybody's wishes, but she held back. All sorts of strangers were there and she was not, and she needed them to do her a favor. "Please," she said urgently, "could you whisper in my mother's ear that I am coming home? Please tell her that Anna is on her way."

She waited for her plane at Logan, watching the digital clock atop the monitor screens. Whenever the numbers added up to thirteen, she looked away. Twenty-four hours? Her mother had been in the hospital for a full day and night? Of course, Anna had expected her mother's body to give out, the inoperable aneurysm to rupture, but she had not expected that her own body would betray her.

During the last twenty-four hours, Anna had eaten and walked her dog, and laughed, and gone to class and watched television and slept, and not once, not even once, had she felt even a tiny pang of that terrible pain in her mother's brain from two thousand six hundred six miles away.

Anna was the family worrier, a human lightning rod. Any flash of trouble that happened to her mother or her brother always rippled through her instantly, painfully racking her body with headaches or chills or asthma attacks. If her mother lost her balance stepping down from the pulpit of her church in Los Angeles on a Sunday morning, then at that exact moment, Anna rolled over in her sleep and fell out of bed onto the cold floor in Boston. If her brother, Luke, had the wind knocked out of him during football practice on a Friday afternoon, Anna doubled over in statistics class, her chest tight, struggling to breathe. This was simply the truth. And she counted on that personal emergency alarm system to give her clear advance warning—not about what had happened, but more precisely when it happened.

Yet for all practical purposes she was fully prepared to leave her apartment as soon as the hospital called. She had already packed everything she needed. One hanging garment bag had been waiting sullenly at the back of her closet, containing her black dress suit, appropriate funeral attire, pressed and ready to wear, with closed-toe, kitten-heel (church ladies' fellowship–approved) black leather pumps. And in the outside zippered translucent pocket where a belt or scarf should go, there was a packet of original documents: trust and estate files, obituary draft (with the date of death left blank), joint bank account checkbook, power of attorney, guardianship papers for Luke, memorial service program, withdrawal of life support advanced directives—all necessary to give Anna legal authority to handle the end of her mother's life. Every official paper had been written, signed, and notarized when she turned twenty-one almost two years ago.

"All grief comes down to this," her mother said in a sermon, "that we have simply run out of time." This was a sermon designed to comfort all the people who were trying to comfort her when she had been given the news that she had a few months to live before her brain was going to time out. "And not one of us ever gets as much time as we want," she continued, fingering the sparkling green and pink rosary a Sunday School class had made for her. The rosary was the Protestant kind with thirty-three beads, one for each year of Jesus' life. The following week, she would officiate at the funeral of one of those children who made the necklace, who died of kidney cancer when he was only nine beads long. It turned out that she wound up having much more time than they all hoped—two years beyond the three months her doctors had predicted. She was fifty-two years old. But Luke was only sixteen.

Luke! Anna jolted in her seat. What had she done? She had
screwed up the plan. Right after the hospital called, she had called
her brother's cell over and over until he finally answered and told
him to meet her at the hospital. Now she remembered that was the
worst thing she could have told him to do and exactly what their
mother had begged her not to do. Her mother had been so em-
phatic about that.

"Don't let your brother see me after I'm gone," she'd told Anna.
"He'll never get over it."

Anna closed her eyes, remembering how she had so readily ac-
cepted that responsibility, along with all the others. She had felt com-
plimented by her mother's faith in her, that she could handle the
sight of her mother's dead body better than her brother. Her mother
was always reminding them of their differences in age and tempera-
ment, but now, none of that mattered. They were both losing the
same thing. How could anybody get over that?

Luke started to shake even before Grace, his high school athletic
trainer, turned on the air conditioning full blast and instantly freeze-
dried the sweat from practice. She was driving eighty, pushing the
team van to its max, zigzagging in and out of the carpool lane as if it
were made for easy passing. He put his hand on her arm gently, and
she looked at him with alarm, asking him if he needed to stop for
food. He shook his head, silently, as he always did when she asked
this question. She watched him from the sidelines during games,
holding up the high-sugar protein drinks she reserved for him to remind him to check himself. Every thirty minutes she held the bottles
over her head, regular as clockwork, his own personal time guard.
But she meant well. Her name, Grace, fit her perfectly. She was
graceful enough not to try to talk to him the entire way there, and to
leave him at the entrance, as soon as he told her that his older sister
was meeting him there.

Then he started shaking again as soon as he walked through the front doors of UCLA hospital out of the July heat into another blast of canned cold air. He checked the clock and knew it would be at least another hour before Anna could make it. How could his mother have been here since yesterday and he never knew? He should have figured out something was wrong when she hadn't called him last night.

During summer football camp, Luke had been staying at a friend's house five minutes from school. He had set that up so he would not have to commute an hour on the freeway. Their beach house was a long way from his high school. His mother knew he had not warmed up to the new place. He hated moving. He hated all big changes. And he hated hospitals most of all. They all had that same smell, the smell of group fear and a mixture of pine-based industrial cleaner, wrapped around the locker-room stench of people dripping terror out of their pores. Hospitals were haunted. Ghosts flew around everyone in this place. That's why they needed double doors at the entrance.

He remembered the day he was released from the Juvenile Diabetes wing here, the one some rich movie mogul had built after his kid died. Luke had been brought into the ER three years earlier, straight from his doctor's office, when he had gone there to try to figure out why he was losing so much weight. Even then, he knew he wanted to play football. They took his blood after hearing that he was thirsty all the time, and that he drank Coke and milkshakes to beef up and was still scrawny. He stayed in the hospital for a week because they would not let him leave until they were sure he understood how sick he was. How sick he would always be, and how dead he would be if he did not pay attention to his blood sugar, or BS, as his family started calling it.

On the day he was discharged, Luke and his mother and sister had walked out into the sunshine that was so bright it made tears run down his face. His mother stopped to stand on her tiptoes and hug him, while Anna searched in her purse for a tissue. And he had protested, "Mom, I'm all right. It's just the sun in my eyes. I'm not crying!"

Then, as if that weren't enough of a scene to embarrass the shit out of him, a nurse outside in the courtyard on break spotted his mother's clerical collar.

"Having a rough day, Reverend?" she called out, presuming his mother was leaving the hospital after visiting with some other loser family, not her own.

And his mother had thrown one of her tightest spiral mini-sermon bombs.

"It's always a good day, isn't it, when we can leave here, walking out on our own two legs, breathing fresh air with our own lungs, and going home to our own beds to sleep."

The "own lungs" thing was a nice touch, since the nurse had been smoking. But that memory made him shudder again. Now his mother was at their mercy. He didn't want to see her in here. Anna was supposed to handle this, but she was so many miles away. She had made sure he understood.

"You need to get over to that hospital! Mom needs you. You're twelve miles away and I'm two thousand six hundred six!"

Anna was a numbers freak, and she never said anything important to anybody without comparing numbers. She hated all odd numbers and particularly loved anything ending with two. He should have just let her keep thinking that he was only twelve miles away from their mother if it made her feel better. Instead, he blurted out that he was forty-three miles away in Laguna Beach.

"Shit! Shit! Shit!" she had screamed into his ear.

Anna had inherited their father's fiery temper, and also this odd habit of sneezing and cursing in triplicate, like once was not enough to get the crud out of their systems. It seemed to come with the dark hair and eyes. Luke could just see her twisting her long, ink-black hair around and around her fingers, worrying.

He looked exactly like their mother, fair-skinned, curly blonde hair, except his eyes didn't do that freaky changing-color thing. His were a bright Crayola sky blue that Anna said made him look like an oversized baby angel floating off in a cloud, seeming like he never had a care in the world. She did not mean this in a good way. She had read somewhere that pale eyes were the sign of a person who could not handle physical pain, although she never mentioned that again after watching him prick his finger five times a day and inject himself without so much as a whimper. She could not stand the sight of even a tiny drop of blood. She did everything else possible to help him back then. He would never forget it. That was where her calculator brain kicked in because she always knew exactly how to measure what he needed to eat. He felt almost normal when she was around.

He walked to the information desk and gave the clerk his mother's name. She gave him the red ICU visitor's badge. He did not want to "visit" his mother in this place. He wanted to remember her the way she looked when his class had gone down to the Rescue Mission for a community service day. She had smiled radiantly at him and his buddies when they came through the back door and helped unload a truck of free food. She always looked so great, like a regular mother, when she wasn't wearing those ugly minister's robes. Her hair was soft and kind of mussed around her face, and her cheeks flushed pink from working the soup-kitchen detail. Misery and despair had always looked good on her. All his buddies commented on how beautiful she looked that day. She was model-thin, but he knew that wasn't necessarily a healthy sign. She looked her best when her life was a total disaster, when everybody else's mother would be pounding down the Grey Goose and slurping up tubes of cookie dough as chasers. But not his mother. The heavier the shit piled on, the more his mother lightened up.

When his parents had separated, five years before, his mother had lost twenty-five pounds in that month between Thanksgiving and

Christmas. After that, he could lift her off the floor. He liked to do that because it always made her laugh out loud, a sound he loved and one he thought he would never hear again after she had gotten the terrible news about the ticking time bomb in her brain. No surgeon in the world seemed to be able to figure out how to fix it before it exploded.

When the elevator opened, he saw his mother's name in big block letters on the whiteboard at the nurse's station—Green, M., Bed Number 402—but there was no place to sit. Then a male nurse came toward him in the hallway, holding out papers for him to sign. He had a big green ribbon on his jacket, that fucking puke green.

Luke hated the color green. Everybody at the church was always giving his family presents in all shades of green, as if this were a brand-new idea, as if their whole house didn't look like Kermit the Frog lived there. Luke stared at the green ribbon and the words underneath. Lasting Legacy Organ Transplant Team.

It was over. They were coming to take the only parts of his mother that she had not already given away. He could not look at the Green Ribbon man again. His stomach started churning, and there was that tin-can taste in his mouth.

"Please call my sister," he said, holding out his cell phone to a woman who was rushing toward him, calling his name. How did she even know his name? She was petite, like his mother, but she ran a great interference block on Green Ribbon man.

He tried to make it to the bathroom but fell to his knees outside the door. "I'm so sorry," he choked out. And she crouched down beside him, an arm around his shoulders, just the way his mother would have done. Luke put his head down between his knees and vomited all over the floor in front of them.

Every time Anna had ever flown home from Boston to Los Angeles, almost always for a family crisis, the weather had stubbornly refused to match her mood. This morning was no exception. Anna leaned her head against the airplane window, its glass cool against her cheek. The sun rose in pinks and yellows below. One more hour before landing. She snapped the plastic shade down, shutting out the dawning beauty of another day.

In movies, it was always raining when a person's heart was breaking, and graveside burial scenes were a study in wet, muddy misery—sobbing people trembling against cold air that would never let up, leaning against one another under shared umbrellas. But she was headed for the relentless California sunshine, where her worst days had always demanded sunglasses and lightweight cotton, even the day her father died.

He'd had a heart attack on a chair lift with his new wife. She jumped off and he slumped over, sideways, with the lift still moving up to the next level. He was pronounced dead at the top of the mountain, which is exactly what he would have wanted. Anna shuddered, thinking about her mother on life support, suspended between worlds, unable to move forward.

Her father had filed for divorce the day before Thanksgiving that year. By the time Anna returned for her first vacation from college, her mother had already found a three-bedroom rental, close enough to the beach to hear the ocean.

"It's not about owning a house, it's about belonging to it," her mother had said. "I told your brother this already. I want you to know that you will always belong in any house where your mother is staying." Again the preaching voice, but even thicker this time, a voice trying too hard to resonate with meaning. Luke, then eleven, had countered with, "Dad keeps the house. But we get Mom." They hadn't seen much of their father after that. They weren't invited to the wedding and it was fine with them.

After that, her mother kept apologizing for taking time away from them to take care of the church. Anna and Luke had never felt neglected. Overlooked sometimes, sure. But they had adapted to living with an extended family of a thousand members who could call their mother day and night. When the brain aneurysm came, with the news that she had only a few months to put her "affairs in order," Anna had dropped out that semester and stayed with her mother and Luke while they waited it out.

During that time, her mother had talked to them about death, with each of them alone, with both of them together, even when they were hanging out with friends. It became an ordinary topic of conversation around their kitchen table. Yes, she and Luke certainly weren't like the other children at school. It got to the point where one time a bunch of Luke's friends were over and they started talking about the best way to die. Most wanted to die in their sleep. Of course, Luke had already given this a lot of thought and he was much more specific. He wanted to die in his sleep on Christmas Eve, after eating every sweet thing he ever wanted.

"That's exactly how it is, sweetie," their mother had exclaimed, clapping her hands together. "That is how every death really is, no matter what the circumstances. We are all headed to Christmas morning—just taking different ways and amounts of time to get there."

But their mother didn't die on schedule. Instead, she gained weight and grew stronger. The headaches and seizures disappeared and the aneurysm stopped growing. Her mother told Anna to go back to college, that everything would be fine.

The plane lurched suddenly as they prepared to land. Anna hated turbulence. She grabbed her set of keys, the weight in her hands feeling solid as a prayer book, a symbol of her mother's faith. Anna was not sure she believed in God, but she did believe in her mother, and as long as she was still on this earth, Anna felt anchored somehow.

She closed her eyes and tried to remember the sound of her mother's voice, which carried all the way to the farthest pew and the deafest person sitting in it. The last time Anna heard her preach, the sermon had focused on Jesus' last words, not on the cross but at

Passover the night before, when he was eating and drinking with his friends and in no physical pain. "Love one another as I have loved you." The Great Commandment.

She remembered her mother's last words to her, the ending of every conversation they had. Love each other with all your hearts.

Luke was changing into the blue hospital scrubs that the lady chaplain had given him when he heard his cell beep with a new message. Thank God Anna was on her way. The lady chaplain was waiting for him outside the bathroom.

Luke said, "My older sister will be here soon. And I promised her that I wouldn't go in to see my mother until she got here. We will do this together."

She put her hand on his arm. "Would you like me to go in and say some prayers in your place?"

"Surrogate praying? That works?"

"Surrogate praying," she said, laughing. "I'll have to remember that one."

"Look, the deal here is . . . well . . . my mother is a minister, too, like you. So you gotta know that she's already had a shitload—sorry—tons more prayers said for her by more people than you can imagine. And not to be disrespectful or anything . . . but it's pretty clear what good it's done her. You know?"

She said she understood perfectly. She was pretty in that soft way his mother was pretty, and she had kind eyes. She showed him into a small room that had only two chairs in it, with a bunch of Bibles and grief booklets on the table. The lady chaplain promised she would bring Anna there. So at least they could regroup before they faced seeing their mother, in her OOPS state. Object of Pity. Object of Prayer. Same thing.

He was so tired of all that bullshit. It had been so weird seeing his mother go from being the church's pathetic prayer-chain Object of

Pity to being a walking, talking miracle. And the whole church decided to take credit for it. Well, then they should've taken the blame for that poor kid who died of cancer at nine years old. They had been praying for him too.

Luke had talked about that with his mother. He was glad she had lived longer and everything, but what was the deal about God answering some prayers and not others? Even his mother agreed.

"Oh, sweetie, I've got lots of questions like that to ask when I get the chance. But the number one on my list is about God's timing. I just never understood why we couldn't all die at one time. Go up in a cocoon kind of spaceship together, like in that movie, except nobody has to be left behind. I hate these staggered departures. That is what makes death so hard to handle, makes us suffer so much."

She was right. He realized how much easier it would've been if his mother and father had died together. One big clean cut and one gaping wound, only one grief bandage to rip from his heart. It was going to be awful. Instant orphan. God, he hated that part. He would never escape the oops looks. His mother hated the oops looks, too.

When he was in the Diabetes Clinic, he begged her not to put him on the church prayer list. "Do you believe in God, Luke?" his mother had asked him.

He told her he didn't think so. He wasn't as *in her face* about not believing as Anna had been, but still he had to be honest. He didn't believe there was any higher power holding all this shit together down here.

When he was younger, he used to think God worked like centrifugal force worked on that barf-o-rama ride, the one that looked least scary, but nobody explained that the big round, spinning dance floor would drop out from under you. They revved up the engine while everyone went round and round, trying not to throw up all over themselves, and God would push everyone down and back against the wall so they wouldn't fly off. Luke didn't believe that anymore.

When he told his mother this, she said she could certainly see why believing in a God like that didn't make her son feel any better. She gave a sermon about it that Sunday. She didn't mention his name or anything, but she said that it was perfectly fine not to believe in God as long as you believed in love.

"Set me as a seal upon thine heart, as a seal upon thine arm: for love *is* strong as death."

She said that line came from the Bible, Old Testament. King Solomon. It sounded like a line of poetry, but it was the closest thing he knew to a prayer.

He closed his eyes and repeated it over and over to himself. *Love is as strong as death.* Yes, he believed that, just wished Love were even stronger and that death didn't always have to win.

Anna's headache was still excruciating, even after Luke had brought her a Coke and sat with her quietly for a few minutes. It was as if all the thoughts that had left her mother's brain were suddenly trying to pound their way into hers. She looked up when the organ donation guy walked into the room. Her vision was still blurry when she signed the release papers, but she remembered the number he told her. Fifty lives would be changed by her mother's gift. It was a good, solid number.

As soon as the organ guy left, a woman entered. Anna noticed the chaplain badge.

"Would you like to go in with us?"

"No."

"No?" Luke turned toward her.

Anna answered the chaplain. "My mother didn't want us to see her this way."

She was surprised when Luke left his chair to hug the chaplain, leaning over to wrap his arms around her. In a flash, Anna remembered her mother's reaction to her father's quick remarriage. "Women grieve. Men replace."

Anna stood beside Luke, waiting.

"I'm just a phone call away," the chaplain said, smiling softly, handing Luke her card.

"BS, Luke," Anna said. "Now."

The chaplain looked at her with alarm, but Luke got it. He nodded and pulled his glucose meter from the plastic bag that contained his sweaty sports clothes. "BS at seventy . . ." he stammered, after jabbing at his finger. It was actually seventy-five, but he caught himself. "Seventy-four, Anna. I'm okay."

"No, that's on the low side," she frowned. "Time for food. Right now. Let's get out of here and get you something to eat." She began pulling him toward the elevators.

"What about Mom?" Luke's voice cracked. "We just leave her here?"

Anna squeezed his hand, holding it tight. She never held his hand, and now she would not let go. They stepped in the elevator, and sister turned around to face brother. They were alone. Together. Which suited her fine.

"Luke," she said quietly. "You know Mom's not here anymore. You know that, right?"

He nodded, closing his eyes.

"You and I are going to be all right," she whispered. "I promise."

"How could we ever be all right again?"

"Because we knew this was coming, and we have a plan."

"Sure. And Mom always said God had a plan. Well, so far, his plan sucks."

"I couldn't agree more," she answered. "That's why we are coming up with our own plan."

And now he was the one who would not let go of her hand.

In the cab, she took a closer look at her brother. He'd become strikingly handsome, had lost the baby fat in his face, revealing their mother's high cheekbones. He must have grown another two inches since she last saw him.

"So, what's the plan?" he asked, his face so much like their mother's—open, trusting, and full of expectation.

"Exactly what I said we were going to do. Go get you something to eat. Mickey D's has a new snack wrap that will balance out the carb load perfectly. I calculated it already. Just leave out the sauce."

His eyes grew wider. "We're going to McDonald's? Are you kidding me? Don't we have to plan something for Mom? Like, you know, a funeral?"

Anna had already figured this out. She hoped he would agree with her.

"Remember what Mom always said about funerals and memorials? She did hundreds of them, and she always said all that stuff was for the living, not the dead." Her voice started to crack on the last word, but she kept talking. "Anyway, my plan is to let the church people put the service together. I'll give them the same instructions Mom gave me. All we have to do is show up. Remember, that's what Mom said God wanted most from us? Just to show up?"

"Yeah, I remember." Luke's shoulders relaxed.

Anna smiled. "So, Little Brother, it's Christmas morning."

"Yep," he said, "and Mom and Dad got there ahead of us, like they always did. But we better take a long-assed damn time to get there."

She sighed, relieved. She loved that he said "we," and that it was clear to him, if nothing else was clear, that wherever they went now, it would be together.

The Viewing Room AUGUST

Age has no bearing in the viewing room. No matter how old and grown up, every person pays the price of a child's admission ticket. They come here with hearts and minds and souls as unformed and pliable as play dough. Their emotions, thoughts, and spirits are wide open to changing shape for the rest of their lives. Everyone's faith is at high risk of devastation in the viewing room.

Some might say they invite and even welcome the loss of the illusion. They approach the viewing room as if it were a spiritual boot camp, a rite of passage that, once passed, proves their maturity. They might say that they come here to let go of their childlike belief that life never ends. They say they need closure and that only a close-up picture of death in its fresh, permanent reality can offer such closure. But they are underestimating the excruciating pain involved when hope is shut down, like having one's heart crushed in a vise. Not one person has ever come to the viewing room a second time. Nobody would choose this again.

It is toughest on the very young. They are still clinging to breakable theologies inherited from their parents that shatter easily under duress, like all secondhand dreams. They go into that room already knowing that adults can tell these giant lies and get away with it—that maybe like Santa Claus and the Easter Bunny and the Tooth Fairy, this Death thing is the biggest fake-out of all. They are ill prepared to see raw reality without the aid of a camera to soft-filter the sharp image of a corpse.

They are living in a cinematic world that conspires with their parents to extend the fantasy of endless life. In movies, in videogames, in action television series, even in the so-called reality dramas, death is staged and acted out in carefully designed scenes. The original life might end suddenly, but in the staged wars reinvented as a spectator sport, characters are given extra lives. On the big and small screens, the dead always come back wearing their same clothes, their same confident grins, looking as if they have been out for a quick smoke behind the school gymnasium. The trick is all about pulling off the charade that dying is an old person's game, and that the young will stay young as long as they can opt to take their ball and move to a happier field of play.

[THE PROBLEM OUTSIDE]

It was a hot, muggy day with the stifling kind of heat one would expect in Manhattan, New York, but not in Manhattan Beach, California. The heat started the morning slowly like a transient, loitering outside the etched-glass seashell-motif double doors of the exclusive boutique hotel Sea Star. The blast of scorched air shocked the wealthy tourists as they walked out, mocking their five-hundred-dollar-a-night vacation habit. All day long the heat slid up and down the cobalt-blue-tiled streets, leisurely sucking up every snatch of ocean breeze as it went, and then after sunset, laid down flat across the chilly waters of the Pacific. There it stayed sulking steamily through the night, making the round aquarium building at the end of the pier look like a constantly boiling-over teakettle.

The high-end property sales of the mansions in all three sections of prime Manhattan Beach real estate were suffocating. There was the Hill section with panoramic ocean views, the Sand Section with white water views, and the Tree Section with no views, and no trees either for that matter, just streets named after lovely leaf-bearing trees, like Magnolia, Dogwood, and Pine, all grown elsewhere. They gave nostalgic value to the human transplants from parts of the country where the namesake trees stay rooted in their native soil. It would have made more sense to name the streets after the various types of local palm trees. However, names such as Pygmy, Cabbage, and Fishtail, although botanically accurate, would have done little to promote the elegant landscape of that oxymoronic advertising myth, the *Mini-Estate*.

Despite the vast quantities of cash poured into the foundations, very few of these cavernous, overbuilt homes were air-conditioned. This was not due to lack of foresight or planning but entirely due to inflated pride, the bragging rights to cool sea breezes in perpetuity. The homeowner's ego springs eternal. A cool sanctuary awaited the wives of these hot houses, however. They could break out from under the tyranny of the relentless sunshine into the cool darkness of movie matinee land. Tree Section, Hill Section, and Sand Section mothers united and rebelled against the common enemy of the mid-day heat. They also came together to satisfy secret cravings for giant boxes of candy and greasy buckets of popcorn and to swallow huge gulps of artificially sweetened iced tea with artificially preserved air.

Today was Monday, so they came in shifts according to the ages of their children because Monday was nanny's second day off. The nannies, live-in or not, must always stay over Saturday night because it is the parents' obligatory romantic-dinner-date night. Even after returning home, the couple sneaks stealthily down the hall without checking on their sleeping children. Then, following the prescriptive advice of the best marital therapists, they lock the master bedroom door, bribing the nanny with double-time pay to respond to any whimpering voices crying out in the wilderness of the children's wing of the house.

By Monday morning, after twenty-four hours of sweltering air drenched with the separation anxiety tears of infants, every family member was eager to run out the front door. First, the fathers escaped to work in air-conditioned buildings on the West Side. Next, the older kids biked their way down to the beach, to surfing or Junior Lifeguard camp, heeding the seductive siren's call of the waves. And, finally, the mass exodus was completed when the mothers and babies rushed off to that cash cow of entertainment—the *Monday Morning Mommy Movie*.

They flocked to the most recently released tear-jerking chick flick, or whatever was playing, not even bothering to check the title.

They huddled down together, flesh-filled front packs worn proudly across their puffed-out chests like battle medals for heroism on five-star generals. These swaddled forms, wrapped in neon-bright summer colors of lime green and hot pink, actually glowed in the dark, squirmy phosphorescent cocoons, while the bodies of the mothers, covered in the stain-resistant mommy uniform of dark-colored cotton, soft, stretchable, recycled yoga and Pilates clothes, faded into the dark.

The mothers luxuriated in the invisibility, settling down into it, grateful for the warm comfort of tantrum-tolerant company. They staked birthright claims to that theater for the next two hours. Technically speaking, other people, not baby-weight-bearing people, were allowed to pay for a ticket and sit down and watch the same movie, but they would enter that sacred nesting ground at great risk of being reported to mall security as a potential child abductor or possible pedophile. One does not wander by mistake into Monday Morning Mommy Movies more than once in a lifetime.

Henrietta shrewdly timed her arrival at the theater as the Mommy swarm was leaving. They buzzed noisily by her, in a heat-wavy blur like a desert mirage. A ghost of her road-not-taken life rose up before her for a moment. She was in her early thirties, but she felt so much older, as if the life of a housewife and mother had passed her by. She had been up for two nights in a row, covering for another chaplain who was home with a family emergency. The Manhattan Beach theater was her preferred way to detoxify. It was a self-medicating decompression chamber that she sleepwalked through after brutal back-to-back-to-back shifts. Tired as she was, exhausted in heart, mind, spirit, and body, she was not yet ready to be alone in her apartment, which was only a fifteen-minute drive farther south in Redondo Beach. She was suffering from an acute bout of compassion fatigue and needed the antidote of movie life.

She went to the end of a line of at least twenty women. This was the second shift of matinee mothers, a serene group of golden-skinned, exquisitely maintained aging beauties. They were in their late forties and early fifties, sleek retired thoroughbreds, done with the sloppy baby business, now free to prance about in light-colored clothes again, showing off their buffed, airbrush-tanned, long limbs. They wanted to be seen. They were fighting the invisibility that shrouded a woman of middle age in Los Angeles. They were caricatures of their former selves, breasts enhanced, hair and lashes extended, lips plumped like dying trout, wrinkles filled in, making their skin so smooth that the sunlight bounced off their shiny faces. And after all that effort to look their best, they had ended up looking exactly alike, clearly having been remade by the same cosmetic surgeon.

She watched them with interest but not envy. The glittering paraphernalia of their fashion habits, their cosmetic surgery habits, or their tennis and golf habits had never seduced her. She did long for one thing that they had at their leisure: disposable income. Not for the luxury of spending it, but for the luxury of giving it away. If she had access to that kind of money, then philanthropy would be the high that would keep her locked in a dead marriage.

"Sure is a bit hot to be waiting outside here in line, isn't it?"

The woman directly in front of her turned around. She was older, silver-haired, with a crocheted coral shawl around her shoulders and lipstick that matched. She smiled at Henrietta, a kindred spirit who did not belong in this group any more than Henrietta did.

Henrietta was well aware that her image would take up an entire corner of the "What's wrong with this picture?" page in those dentist's office magazines for children. Everything about Henrietta was at least one design detail from the prototype. She had tried new looks, but she never seemed to get the memo about when certain trends were over, when to stop matching the color of her fingernails to her toes or to stop highlighting and start lowlighting, that kind of thing. Fortunately, at divinity school she was among a group of women, over half of the student body, who cared as little about all that as she did. It was such a relief to worry about what she was thinking and believing instead of what she was wearing. It turned out to be far easier to grasp a systematic theology than it had been to grasp a sense of style.

Henrietta bought the ticket to whatever movie they were planning to watch because it was handed to her automatically at the admission counter and she was too tired to make a decision for herself anyway. Longing to sit down, she skipped the concession stand and grabbed a place in the very back row, aisle seat, closest to the door. A few years ago, she had been in a theater during an earthquake aftershock, dead center, trapped. She would not repeat that experience of crushing, panicked humanity pressing upon her from all sides. The other women spread out and took their time to choose their seats. Each one sank into her seat with a sigh loud enough to be heard above the pumped-up volume of the trailers.

Henrietta was still listening to the way other people were breathing. She needed a loading dose of movie watching, two, maybe three movies, before it was safe for her to drive home. These were not hospice patients on morphine drips whose agonal, stop-and-start breathing was the cue for her to begin the prayers for the dying in her Pastoral Care Book of Worship. No, she was counting the breaths of healthy, vibrant Manhattan Beach mothers. These were world-class competitive breathers, practiced-their-pranas-until-perfect Champions of Exhalation. Their sighs were loud not because their hearts were heavily packed with cares and woes but because their abdominal cores were heavily packed with muscle.

Once, Henrietta had tried exercise as a remedy to an all-nighter of seeing dead people. She used a friend's guest pass to a twenty-four-hour gym near the hospital. As soon as she went inside, she froze at the entryway, a paralyzed pillar of salt like Lot's wife. Looking through the picture window at the frantic activity inside, she could see only the backward reflection of the world she was trying to forget. The flashing red lights of the cardio machines morphed into ICU heart-lung monitors; the personal trainers with their clip-boards and measuring tapes were medics taking vitals; the grim, flushed faces looking back at them were patients hearing once again the inevitable diagnosis that life was a terminal condition.

Surrounded by all these toned, endorphin-haloed women, Henri-etta wondered if she should try again. Aerobic activity had worked miracle cures for the other chaplains. Each had found a ritual of exorcism for the haunted mornings after the on-call nights. Father Barry surfed in Hermosa Beach five minutes from here, a sight Hen-rietta had been tempted to try to catch on her way back home, but their schedules never coincided. Rabbi Marc played pickup basket-ball at his local JCC in the valley. And Maurice, her closest friend on the Spiritual Care Staff, confessed that he pole-danced at a Santa Monica strip bar owned by a friend who opened it up early just for him. She would love to see that, just once.

The movie was starting, an Indian film with English subtitles. It began with an aerial view of a wedding party, spirals of danc-ers trailing ribbons of juicy colors that undulated slowly across the screen. The celebrants were singing in a language she did not need to understand to hear the delicious carbonated ecstasy in their voices. She settled back to take it all in and drifted into sleep.

A man shouting a question woke her up.

"Is there a doctor in the house? Please, is there a doctor in the house?"

Henrietta had never actually heard anyone say this except in a book or a play. So she assumed it must be coming from the movie. But it was not. The screen was blank. The theater was no longer dark. A spotlight beamed down on the seating area from the pro-jection room, its white-hot fluorescence as harsh and glaring as an operating-room light. Her eyes watered. When she looked around, she could see the other women were also blinking back tears, their hands cupped against their foreheads in makeshift visors, as if they were standing in direct sunlight.

"Then, does anybody know CPR? We have a problem outside!"

The man shouting was the same man who gave them their tickets at the window. He was standing just inside the doorway, next to Henrietta's seat at the back of the theater. He was short and stocky, his round face glistening with sweat, and he was holding a thin notebook against his chest with both hands. The title in red block letters was *Employee Emergency Manual*. He started to fan himself with it under the hot lights. Most of the women shook their heads silently, but the older lady who had spoken to Henrietta in line rushed forward and ran into the lobby with him. They all followed.

Each woman screamed, one by one, as the problem outside came into clear view through the double glass outer doors of the theater. It was a faded pink mummy-shaped sleeping bag, child-sized, slithering on the concrete sidewalk right next to the exit doors. It looked like a three-foot slug in shape, and there were dark red wet stains on both ends. There was no way to get to the parking lot without having to step around it.

The stench of vomit and feces was almost unbearable. No wonder those women were racing to their cars. She reached into her purse, squeezed the bottle of citrus aromatherapy oil, drenched her fingers and rubbed them across the end of her nose. The relief was instantaneous. The rest of the women covered mouths with their hands, their groans muffled as they made a run for it.

Henrietta watched the shape writhing on the concrete. The ticket man was standing behind her, now propping the emergency manual over his face like a tent, giving him a little pocket of personal air space.

"Did you call 911?" she asked him.

"Yes. As soon as I saw that car screech into the lot and dump it like trash. They stole the skateboard, yanked it right off the poor sucker." He started to cough and had to take the manual from his face. Then he pinched his nostrils together. His face was still flushed deep red. "But I got the plate numbers of those assholes. Oh, shit. Excuse me!" He was gagging. Henrietta stepped a few feet away, even though it was a relatively regular occurrence in her profession.

If he vomited on her, it would be the third time somebody had done that in the last day and a half. He covered his mouth and rushed back into the theater.

She looked over at the pink sleeping bag. It had stopped moving, and in its stillness, it definitely looked as if it could be a small human being. Oh, God, please don't let it be a dead little girl. She could not bear this. Not again. As if in direct answer to her prayers, a head with wisps of silky white hair, and then a gray face, slid out from the vomit end, hitting the cement with a dull thump. The woman with the coral shawl knelt next to the body. She had slipped her shawl, folded like a pillow, underneath what must have been the head. Then she peeled back the skin. No—it could not be human skin that she was peeling like an onion!

Henrietta rubbed her eyes. She must have been having some kind of autopsy flashback. She cried out as the aromatherapy oil stung her corneas. How many times had she done this and still hadn't learned? The woman looked up and motioned for her to come closer to help. Henrietta's eyes and nose were streaming now, but she walked over and knelt down beside them.

It was not skin but a gray wool ski mask that she had peeled off. The woman rolled it up and back very slowly, starting at the neck. Large Adam's apple, white whiskered chin, a crumpled mouth, sunken in over toothless gums, bruised dark purple cheeks, fleshy pug nose, and a high forehead. His skin was pale with a yellowish tinge, crisscrossed with broken red capillaries. Dark blood poured out of the top of his head where the hat had been, soaking the shawl. It was an old man's head on a child's body. A dwarf?

"I'm afraid it's too late. He's gone," the woman said, glancing up at Henrietta. She was pressing two fingers against the right side of his neck and then the left, searching for the pulse of a carotid artery. "Brain injury. Probably from hitting the pavement when they dumped him here."

"Doctor?" Henrietta asked.

"Nurse," she answered. She unzipped the sleeping bag and took it out from under the body. He was not a dwarf. A double amputee. And then she leaned closer to the man, almost nose to nose, like a lover leaning in for a kiss, and pushed his eyelids closed with her thumbs.

"Oh, good-bye, sweetheart. I'm so sorry," the nurse said, cradling his head in her arms now, his whole body in her lap.

Where was that ambulance? Henrietta got up and went over to tap on the window of the ticket counter. The man was talking on the phone. He opened the window and told her that the ambulance had been canceled. The new city health regulations allowed the first responders to pronounce death in the field if a doctor or nurse was at the scene. Henrietta already knew about these new regulations because they had been a saving grace to hospitals, sparing time and money in the understaffed, overflowing, emergency rooms, where, under the old laws, all bodies were transported for the sole purpose of pronouncing death before arriving at the mortuary. So the problem stayed outside.

It would be another twenty minutes before the police would arrive, he told her. They were dealing with another case. "It must be an L.A. Revenge Day."

"What?"

"Oh, the local surf gangs do a shout-out when they want the beaches cleaned up and the police aren't doing enough. Those poor homeless people really put a damper on their good time. They think they own the beach, the golden boys. So they send the word out, you know, Facebook, Twitter, all the regular channels, and announce another L.A. Revenge Day."

"And then what happens?"

"Well, I guess they get big points when they play whack-a-mole with the drunk bums sleeping on the beach and drop them off somewhere else. They call it B and D day, for 'bump and dump.'"

"Oh, my God. It's a regular thing?"

"Yeah, it's starting to be. And they may be teenagers, but they are meaner than shit. Last L.A. Revenge Day was all about fire. They poured rubbing alcohol over a couple of those poor suckers and threw a lighted match on top. Called that trick the 'Spurn and Burn.'"

Now Henrietta was feeling queasy. She looked back and saw that the nurse had wrapped the dead man back up and covered his face with the bloody shawl. She joined Henrietta in the restroom, where they both washed their hands for several minutes in silence. Then they sat in the air-conditioned lobby and talked. Ellie was the nurse's name. She had come to the movie to escape the heat because she had MS and needed the air conditioning. She wasn't a nurse any longer. She facilitated a grief group of mothers who had lost children in the last six months. She was hoping the movie would be a distraction as well. What a disaster! She was not prepared to face another death, even that of a stranger. But when she saw the sleeping bag, she had a horrible flashback. It was exactly like the one that her daughter, Mandy, had died in.

Mandy had been camping with her Girl Scout troop in the San Bernardino Mountains and had died of a heart attack at thirteen. Congenital defect, no symptoms, no way to have prevented it. When Ellie saw that slithering pink sleeping bag, she ran as fast as she could, as if to make sure that it wasn't her little girl, as if she had gotten a second chance to save her. But it wasn't anybody's little girl. It was a sick, tired, old man, hopefully drunk enough not to have felt his skull crack when they dumped him at the theater. And the worst part, she confessed to Henrietta, the worst part was that she had been relieved to see that it was an old man and not somebody young.

"Me too," Henrietta replied.

"Is that terrible of us?" Ellie said, finally, touching Henrietta's arm and looking into her face. It was the first moment she had taken a breath from telling her story to shift her eyes from the body, as if she needed to keep her eyes on it so it would not get away. "That poor man out there, poaching in that heat outside, all alone, while we still sit and watch, like it's just another movie."

Henrietta put her hand on hers. "Actually, I think you were wonderful to go out there when nobody else would. And especially after everything you have been through. I wish my mother were alive so she could have been part of your group," Henrietta said.

She told Ellie about her brother's death, run over in a crosswalk while trying to catch a bus, the sorrow of the accidental killer, and her mother dying of cancer a short time afterward. They talked about how grief can wear a person down, so that cancer has a better chance to win. Ellie was seventy-seven, the age Henrietta's mother would have been. Henrietta wanted to crawl inside the warmth of her voice and stay snuggled there.

"Your faith must have been a great gift during that time," Ellie said.

Henrietta paused. She liked this woman, and she wanted to tell her the truth—that she had lost her faith in God when her brother was killed. She had officiated at his funeral, but the words were hollow, and she had woken up that morning with this emptiness that was horrifying. What good was a minister who no longer believed? Or worse, a minister who was pretending to believe? She had no right to lead a church. The hospital was the only place where she found people constantly filled with the chronic ache of doubt. And in this strange way, it had helped make her feel less alone in her despair. Ellie was looking at her, waiting for her answer.

"Actually, I think that faith comes and goes in waves, like the ocean. And unfortunately mine was at a very low tide at the time I needed it most," Henrietta said.

"Oh, yes. I do know how that can happen. I have seen it with my group, I am so sorry to say. And I'm guessing the tide still hasn't come in yet," Ellie said.

"How did you know? What did I do?"

"Oh, honey, I'm not judging, believe me, but it was what you did *not* do. You didn't say a word of prayer over that man's body, and I know you saw the cross tattooed on his arm."

Henrietta nodded. She had seen it but had hoped that Ellie had not noticed her failure. She suddenly felt all the weight of another thing she hadn't done in two days—sleep.

"You know, we can't even buy a break, can we?" Ellie said, in that false cheerful voice that must come with nursing training. "Well, that was the last thing any of us needed today, wasn't it?"

Henrietta shook her head. Tears were forming at the back of her throat now, real tears of sorrow, not the stinging reaction to the aromatherapy oil. But she was feeling most sorry for all of them, not the man who had died, because his suffering was over. It was a cruel, sick joke that they had come to this movie trying to avoid the specter of death and had still had it thrown at their feet.

Ellie saw Henrietta's tears and reached over and patted her arm. "You know, I haven't practiced nursing since Mandy died. I didn't want to go over and examine that body, to tell you the honest truth. I wanted to run home. But I just couldn't."

Henrietta understood perfectly. Ellie could not leave him alone, and Henrietta couldn't leave Ellie alone. They couldn't leave the problem outside because they were the kind of people who always take the problem inside, where it made itself at home and went everywhere they went. Dead bodies had become so much a part of Henrietta's life that after the police arrived and took everyone's statements, and they were cleared to leave, she stayed outside waiting. And when the mortuary car arrived and loaded the pink sleeping bag in, Henrietta waved good-bye, as if it could wave back. And then she turned around, went back to the theater, and asked to see the next show. And the man, bless his heart, gave her the ticket for free.

The Viewing Room SEPTEMBER

There are as many views of death as the people who come here to view it. When death is pronounced inside a hospital, the number of viewers multiplies. When that hospital is located in Los Angeles, where thousands of cultures and races and religions intersect, the viewing room is a cauldron of multifaith ritual and ceremony. Time is elastic in this room. Five minutes looking at the dead body of a little girl who was crushed that morning under a falling tree branch while playing in her kindergarten courtyard can seem like five years—one for every year of her life. There is no clock in this room, and chaplains are told not to look at their watches, but none of them would do so anyway.

Chaplains move at a different pace than the other staff, often coming into a patient's room as the last doctor and nurse are leaving. The ancient Greeks had two words for time. The first and more ordinary was *chronos*, chronological time, the time of the gigantic railway clock. The God of this time, Chronos, ate his own children, just as time gets the best of us all. But chaplains are also called to work on the other time, *kairos* time, sacred time, with no ties to the numbers of seconds or hours. The time to die, the time to give birth, and the time to let go of one's dead child is set on *kairos* time.

Is it only the living who are allowed to view the body, or can the dead view themselves? Many believe that the spirit stays close to the body because their religious writings have spelled out how carefully the body must be treated before burial. Others have formed their beliefs from what they call a near-death experience, and swear that they saw themselves in the recovery room or operating room, hovering up in the ceiling corner with a panoramic view of the chaos of heroic measures taken to revive them. Or is attendance at one's own death optional? There would be those who would hang on to their precious bodies until the last possible moment, especially in Los Angeles, where the body is often its own temple of worship.

But when does that moment arrive, exactly? Does the spirit flee its cage when the breathing stops or when the heart stops or when the brain stops? All organs have ceased to function by the time the body comes into the viewing room. Yet the question of when life begins and ends has not been resolved. The bitter controversy over these differing beliefs continues to divide the faiths, turning them against each other, causing splintering and rebellions, renunciations and excommunications, and even murder, in their God's name. But here the war has ended and the body has ceased to be a battleground. In the viewing room, there is peace paid with the highest price, but blessed peace at last.

[BLOOD RULES]

The sound of his hospital pager shaking his nightstand stirred him from sleep. He waited a few minutes before looking at the message. He had this uneasy feeling in his chest, as if the air was going in one direction, out of his lungs but not back in, no matter how many calm breaths he tried to take. He knew it was the anniversary re-action, disguised like a heart attack every year, but in those first few moments of waking up on September 11, it knocked the wind out of him every time. It had been twelve years to the day since Maurice ruined his career when he gave one wrong answer. He could still re-member the question, word for word, and years later, he would have to answer it the same way, no matter what it cost.

"Which commandment has given you the most trouble in your faith journey?"

This was the question that the ordination committee had asked Maurice, and he had answered without hesitation.

"Thou shalt not kill," he had said.

It was the truth, and the truth was supposed to set you free. As it happened, he was freed from receiving the title of Reverend. He would never be a licensed minister until he proved to this committee that he possessed a systematic personal theology that embraced him and all those members of his future flock who would look to him for inspiration and leadership in times of utmost suffering.

That had been over a decade ago, and he would never stop pay-ing for his honesty. He had been up for ordination at this exact time of year, the second week of September 2001, only days after the 9/11 disaster. The temples and the churches and the mosques had been overflowing with people, many of them coming to their houses of worship for the first time in years, looking for God. They were also looking to God's spokespeople, the priests, ministers, rabbis, and imams, for an explanation. His ordination committee looked exhausted, their faces gray with fatigue. Each of them had been overwhelmed with questions they could not answer. Where was God in the midst of all this suffering? How could the murderers say they worshipped the same God, a kind and loving and forgiving God, and kill all those people in the name of religion?

But that had not been the reason Maurice had answered the question in that way. In fact, when the towers fell and he went to the Unitarian church where he was on the staff to open up the doors to those lost souls, he did not share their outrage. Yet he was also not in the same frame of mind as the senior and assistant ministers, who were lighting the chalice of peace and gathering various inspirational passages and poetry about forgiveness and peaceful hearts. He was thinking to himself, *Welcome to my world*. He did not dare express this out loud to anybody. And today, twelve years later, he was ashamed to realize that as the world acknowledged this anniversary, he felt terribly selfish that it was the sharp pang of personal loss that hit him before he remembered that the world had suffered. Wherever his faith journey led him, he knew that he would wrestle with this commandment for his entire life. It was the only commandment he was tempted, every day, to break. Just once.

Maurice wanted to kill the man who had raped and tortured and killed his mother.

He had hoped the state would do that for him, but the monster (how could he be human, since he did not have a soul?) was arrested for another gruesome murder in Arizona, and the death penalty had been abolished a year before his trial.

At the time of his mother's death, Maurice had been a figure skater touring with a national ice show. He was rehearsing when he got the news. His mother had had tickets to see him perform for the first time in a major performance in Los Angeles that night. Instead, she was assaulted in her motel room. He never went back to the show, or to the ice, again. His mother had always wanted to be a minister and had never had the chance. So he had used his inheritance from her to pay for a graduate program at Pacific School of Theology, the most liberal divinity school in the country. Then he had spent a year on the Santa Monica church staff, serving as a pastoral counselor and guest preacher. The congregation adored him and had sponsored him proudly for ordination.

And then he had answered that question the wrong way. It was like a spiritual castration, a term he did not use lightly. But lack of ordination did not affect his chaplaincy, where he could perform such sacraments as baptisms and marriages in emergency circumstances. It affected his religious life outside the hospital, when he longed so many times to perform these ceremonies out in the light of day, with people who would live to see the light of the next day.

"And how did you get the call?" the first-year seminary students would ask one another, by way of introduction.

"Oh, I called Him and now I'm still waiting for the call back, where He explains everything," he would say. "I'm in the remedial classes."

They would laugh, thinking he was joking. After all, they had come to divinity school having already found God, their faith at its highest level. It never occurred to any of his classmates that he might be faking it. He remembered the faces of the Ordination Committee members as he told them his mother's story and the shock, then revulsion, and yes, finally, pity for his lost soul.

"It would be better, the next time your application comes up for review," they had advised him, "that you work on forgiveness. We can't accept a theology that does not believe that every soul can be redeemed. Every soul. Even that man who killed your mother. Particularly *that* man. Forgive him first and then come back to us."

When you are fixed, is what they had really meant to say. We do not ordain broken souls. Come back when you are fixed, and then we will give you the license to go out and fix others. He had dreaded going to the senior minister of his sponsoring church to tell him the news of his failure.

Roland was playing solitaire on his computer, something he did every morning to relax into the day. Roland had run the church for forty-five years, had central-casting looks for the part, tall and broad-shouldered, godlike himself, sweep of silver hair, gray-green eyes.

"Roland, I tried my hardest. But I had to answer the questions with the truth. It's not that I have lost my faith in God. It is that I have lost my faith in the goodness of every human soul."

Roland stopped looking at the computer screen and spun his chair around to look at Maurice. His face was impossible to read, smooth and expressionless. Maurice had seen this look before, but only at a distance. This was the face that looked out and over caskets, his memorial-service face. A face that reflected sorrow to the out-side world but filtered it carefully before it got underneath his skin. Behind him, the screen announced his win, and the cards danced and danced, the ace of spades doing a do-si-do with the queen of hearts.

"The only way to find something you have lost, Maurice," he said, "is to go back to the very place you lost it. Not seminary, my dear man. You would not find your faith there, the least likely of all places." He shook his head. "You simply have to follow the rule of losing things and go back to the last place you remember having it. Go to that exact spot, in time and space, and pick it back up again."

And for Maurice, that place was a hospital, where he had last seen his mother in the viewing room. The sight of her had ripped his soul apart. So, over the last twelve years, he was rebuilding his faith in humankind, patient by patient. Besides, Maurice had discovered that the title of Reverend could push away many patients, those who were in recovery from their rigid, judgmental Protestant childhoods. He had seen that happen with the new chaplain, Reverend Henrietta Hooper, even though she was sweet and kind. Perhaps she had the larger handicap because she had lost her faith in God rather than in people. Well, between the two of them, they could make a complete minister. How she had laughed when he told her that. She was such a dear little one.

He believed that the hospital was one of those sacred places where the veil between the physical and spiritual worlds was gossamer thin and almost transparent. He had loved his years there. He had found his place in the world, there, among his own kind, the wounded veterans of private wars.

The Muslim chaplain, Masoud, was conducting an interfaith service in the hospital chapel later this morning, commemorating the day, and Maurice had agreed to take his on-call shift. He turned the television off and dialed into his voice mail. There was already a message from Josie, the director of the Spiritual Care Department. He grimaced at the sound of her voice.

Josie McCully was an imposing woman, a study in gray and purple. She was large-boned, with long gray hair that hung straight down, parted in the center, so that her flat face, devoid of any makeup, looked blank as a screen between steel curtains. She had a wide mouth with inward-turning lips that covered her tiny teeth, like a sock puppet. He could see her gumming her words as he replayed her message over and over so he could write down all the pertinent facts. Josie always swallowed the ends of her sentences, and it wasn't until the end that she ever got to the point, like a name or a phone number.

She had her own kind of uniform, ankle-length flowing skirts (thank God, she spared the world having to look at her tree-trunk legs) and long purple caftans, only royal purple for the self-appointed Miss America of Spirituality. She wafted up and down the hospital corridors, making sure she was seen, wearing layers of purple silken shawls that fluttered around her short neck and thick waist, spreading herself like a bruise. She had not actually visited a regular patient (she would see the celebrities) in the twelve years that Maurice had been there, but she covered hallways, looking as if she had been summoned, as if she were on a desperately important mission of mercy. Almost as wide as she was tall, she was impossible to miss and also impossible to stop because she was surprisingly fast and agile for her size, as quick as the best figure skaters he had known. She was so sure-footed and headstrong, encased in her purple spiritual elegance, that nobody dared stop her to ask for help.

Maurice sighed as he listened to her singsong voice. Josie was ordering him to handle an Emergency Room DOA, a Muslim teenage girl who had died of heat stroke. She had requested the use of the viewing room for the al-Ghusl, the ritual washing before burial. He could not believe what Josie was saying. First of all, the viewing room was not appropriate for that kind of ceremony. The hospital was supposed to call an Islamic mortuary to pick up the body immediately so that it could be buried within twenty-four hours.

But Josie had shortcut the protocol. She had decided to "work at home" today, she mumbled in her message, because she needed to "reclaim" the meaning of 9/11 for herself and mourn in private. Really? Josie had not known anyone who had lived in New York at that time. And besides, who in their right mind dares to co-opt a global disaster? Could he now have dibs on the Holocaust even though he was not Jewish and not alive when it happened?

There was nothing Maurice hated more than the display of spiritual arrogance, not to mention the absolute lack of any cultural competence. The assignment was an insult, not to him, but to the Muslim faith. He was not qualified to assist. Only females attend to the bodies of other females according to the laws of Islam. He would have to call in Henrietta for help. He texted her to meet him outside the viewing room in an hour.

"I don't know anything about this washing-shrouding business! This is really complicated stuff!"

Henrietta was holding up the health care providers handbook on Muslim patients in her right hand. She had the clear plastic bag of the regulated king-sized white shroud sheets pressed against her chest like a bandage. "And I already promised to help Masoud with the chapel service, and I am on the program. Josie put me there because she was working at home . . ."

"Oh, honey, don't get me started on that," Maurice said. "We can divvy up the other historic catastrophes between us later. But we have ten minutes before the patient and her escort arrive here. You're a quick study. Start reading."

Henrietta shook her head. "I can't do it, sweetie. I really can't. The service starts in five minutes and the fliers are posted all over the hospital. There's already an overflow line down the hall outside the chapel."

"Why can't there be at least one other female chaplain in this place?" he asked, already knowing the answer. Henrietta just stood and looked at him. He sighed as he realized what he had to do now. He looked into Henrietta's eyes.

"What goes on in the viewing room stays in the viewing room, right?" he said solemnly.

"Of course. And nothing is ever as it seems in there, anyway."

"True enough. OK, I'll let you go. As a male, I can't touch the body. But I don't want to alarm her friend. So, I need two favors."

Henrietta sighed with relief.

"Thank God. Anything. What?"

"I need all the makeup you have in your bag, to cover my face. I didn't even shave this morning. Then I need you to go up into Josie's office—top file drawer to the right of the door—and bring me back down all those purple god-awful caftans and scarves. Hurry!"

She pulled her under-eye shadow concealer, compact and lipstick from her purse and handed the makeup to him with the al-Ghusl kit. Then she met him in the viewing room bathroom to give him Josie's stash of extra clothes. He glanced at himself one more time in the mirror as he wrapped a lavender satin scarf around his head. His heart clenched at the sight of the ghostly image in the mirror.

He suddenly realized that he was the same age his mother was when she was killed, forty-two years old. Oh, God, he could not afford to think about that now.

There was a knock at the door that made them both jump. Maurice took his badge and placed it carefully under one of the folds of the silk bow so that the top identity line of his name was obscured but the title of chaplain still showed underneath.

"If it's the orderly with the body, please tell him that you will be the one to wait here until the patient's family arrives," he whispered. "I don't want him to recognize me."

Henrietta nodded in agreement, still unable to keep her eyes off his face, as if she no longer recognized him. He went into the small bathroom and shut the door, making sure to keep himself turned away from the mirror.

The girl who came to perform the al-Ghusl did not even look at him. She was laying out the white cloths on the countertop. Then she went into the bathroom to fill up a basin of purification water, and he followed her. He asked her about the death of her friend, in a whisper, so she would not be alarmed by his voice. She was a sixteen-year-old girl. Her name was Najah. Sedigeh, the girl who had collapsed with heat exhaustion on the basketball court, was her teammate. Sedigeh's parents were in San Francisco, and it would take them hours to get here. They had asked Najah to take care of their daughter until they arrived. When Maurice asked how it had happened, Najah told him that the air conditioning in the gym had failed, but the coaches had insisted that the game go on.

"Those coaches should be arrested," Maurice exclaimed when she told him. Najah cowered when she heard him speak out loud, and she rushed back over to her friend, cupping her hands around her ears. He put his hand over his mouth, instantly regretting the words. He knew better than to speak in anger near the body. Muslims believed that the body of a recently deceased person retained all the sensory perceptions of the living. It was simply that during this short time before they were buried, they could not move or communicate. They were suspended in a sacred space and must be shielded by their loved ones from any further stress. It was forbidden to do or say anything that might distress the spirit in its vulnerable state as it hovered close by.

He apologized as he went to her side, careful to whisper now. Najah shook her head. "No, it was not their fault. They were only following the blood rules."

She explained that the official American rules of play for high school basketball were that if an injury occurred that caused bleeding, the player had to leave the court and replace the uniform with a clean one. Sedigeh had sustained a small cut on her chin that had bled one drop, just one drop, onto her shoulder. She did not want to uncover herself in public because even the visiting team's locker room was exposed to non-Muslims. So she had taken the uniform of Najah (who was sidelined with a swollen hamstring) and layered it over the one she was already wearing, so that the red stain could not be seen. It must have been 110 degrees in that gymnasium. Sedigeh had died faithfully, Najah said solemnly. Then she pulled out a small compass, studied it, and carefully moved the gurney toward Mecca.

Maurice stepped back. There were no chairs in the viewing room, a deliberate exclusion to discourage visitors from staying too long, so he sat up on the counter beside the sink that was in the corner of the room. He found himself looking down at Najah and Sedigeh as if watching a play from the balcony.

Najah took great care so that her friend would not feel any pain. Muslims believe that the dead body felt pressure many times more than a living body. For the washing, she wrapped her hands with the smallest sheet of the packet of shrouds, making thick white cotton mittens. After covering the private parts with a winding sheet, she washed the body slowly, every inch, head to toe, three times. Then she peeled off the hand coverings and prepared another clean bowl of water into which she had added drops of perfumed oil. The intoxicating scent of crushed lotus flowers filled the room. Suddenly, she turned to Maurice and pressed a finger to her lips, as if to swear him to silence. He nodded, not even sure what he was agreeing to, and she turned back to her friend.

Najah caressed every inch of the body again, but this time with no cloth barrier between Sedigeh's skin and her own. And it was then that Maurice finally understood the plea for confidentiality. This friendship had its own special secret. Yet Maurice would vouch for her to the family who would come into the viewing room later that night. It would be their only question to him when they saw their child's body. Just like Najah, neither the mother nor the father would shed a tear. The imperatives of the Qur'an absolutely forbade any emotional displays of grief, even from parents over children. They would ask him simply if he had witnessed every part of the preburial ceremony and if it had proceeded according to the precepts of their faith.

Najah took her friend's left hand and placed it on her chest and then moved the right hand to cover it. She leaned over to sprinkle the remaining water over the face first, and her tears fell with the water. Then she combed the perfumed oil through Sedigeh's hair with her fingers until the blue-black long curls glistened and plaited it in three braids. After she had wound the body with the large sheets, she used smaller sheets as ties to bind it closed, above the head, twice around the waist, and below the feet. The sheets of white cotton were very thick and opaque, and the finished effect was more like a cocoon.

She turned back again and motioned him to leave. He knew that he was not allowed to do this under hospital protocol, but as he watched her prostrate herself on the floor, praying next to the body, he knew he could no longer invade this sacred space. And for the first and only time, he broke the viewing room rules. He left a visitor alone with the body. Yet somehow, he knew she was not alone.

When he stood up and walked out, he felt almost weightless, as if the air had lost all its gravitational pull. It seemed as if the entire room was moving, a floating container taking all of them, not just the white cloud at the center, but all three of them to another world. And for a moment, he fervently wished that it were true, that he could accompany this body to wherever it was going, wrapped as a gift, in layers of love.

The Viewing Room OCTOBER

The chaplain must keep careful watch over visitors to ensure that the corpse remains intact and unaffected by its brief stay here. But this requires constant vigilance, open-eyed prayers, and quick deflective actions, because mourners have uncontrollable impulses in the viewing room. Remarkable acts may occur the moment a head is bowed. Many are determined to take something out of the room with them, something more than an intangible, visual memory, something to hold against their hearts. Usually it is a lock of hair, but it can be more substantial than that—a finger, an earlobe, and other appendages deeply personal to the grieving party.

Only authorized hospital staff members are allowed cut-and-paste privileges with the dead. All emotionally unstable visitors—as if there is any other kind in such an insanity-provoking place—are carefully screened for possession of any sharp objects. There is one pair of safety scissors hidden in the bathroom drawer, the rubberized, round-tipped kind that toddlers use for arts and crafts at preschool, incapable of altering the shape of the dead.

Then there are those visitors whose only desire is to follow their beloved as quickly as possible, no matter the destination. For the rest of their lives, they will wish that they had died with the beloved. The popular narratives in stories and films about zombies coming back to reclaim the living do not frighten them. Nothing scares them anymore except the future, now shredded by the jagged piece of despair, lost love.

Ellie could see the Grim Reaper from the parking lot, but she was not going to give him the time of day. She lowered her head and trudged through the entryway of the Torrance Community Center, shoving the ghastly image, both hands pressing against his black torso, so she could get inside. Someone with considerable talent for three-dimensional art had painted the glass door with the classic hooded figure emerging from a gray background fog, the face its usual blank oval of darkness, one empty sleeve cupping the bloodred handle of his perpetually sharpened scythe, the axe end drawn in sparkling silver puff paint. Alarmingly, the other sleeve seemed to reach out of the glass when the door swung closed. Ellie shuddered as she realized the ominous effect this would have on her Mothers' Grief Group. They were meeting in this building in less than half an hour, and she did not have enough antibacterial wipes in her purse to clean off this hellish door. Yes, everyone has to die, but people like her—parents who have outlived a child—did not have to be reminded of the one thing they could never forget. Ellie had hated Halloween since her daughter Mandy died.

She despised everything about it—the iridescent plastic skeletons hanging from palm fronds swaying softly in the ocean breeze; the fake RIP tombstones rising out of eternally spring-green front lawns; stuffed bloody hands sliding out from the back trunks of bright-colored convertibles—all of it. Another lifetime ago, when Mandy was born, she had carefully decorated their rental on a walk street in Manhattan Beach with the few cheerful items she could find: twinkling pumpkin lights outlining the door and a life-sized stuffed fairy godmother figure that held a magic wand in one hand and a huge bowl of apples in the other.

The Manhattan Beach walk streets were considered the safest part of Los Angeles to trick-or-treat, attracting families from miles away because no cars were allowed on the wide concrete paths of the sand section between perfect rows of imitation New England seaside cottages that oddly faced one another rather than the ocean. The houses were incestuously close together due to the premium lot value, some only two feet apart, so that one could hand a tissue to the sneezing next-door neighbor window to window. The great advantage of this demographic at Halloween was to get the most treat for your trick.

It was possible to visit more than a hundred houses in the space of an hour if you could run as fast as your children.

In fact, she soon discovered that walk streets were no more about walking than strollers were about strolling. The walk streets were made for wheels, a constant stream of carless traffic, back and forth: plastic Cozy Coupes, bikes, skateboards, and homeless women with grocery carts full of junk. The relentless scraping of concrete became white noise snuffing out all the other sounds around it, including the laughter of children playing, the tinkling of wind chimes, the roar of the ocean waves only a few short blocks away.

Ellie had finally moved away from all those sounds, taking a job as the on-call nurse in an assisted living facility in exchange for free rent in a handicap-access apartment. She was about the same age as most of the tenants, seventy-seven. She had moved just in time because the heat wave over the past few days had caused her multiple sclerosis to relapse. Her vision blurred and her lower legs numbed out when she was overheated, and even the slightest exertion derailed her, making her unable to see or feel where her feet landed.

At this time of year, the Santa Ana winds reversed the offshore airflow patterns, so that on Halloween the usually divine coastal weather was also under a witch's spell, the beach disguised as desert, the stinging hot dry air filled with ashes from inland brush fires. Everyone looked grief-stricken in this weather, constantly blinking back tears, so her slow-moving clumsiness could be excused as a result of allergy medication. She had never actually told anyone in her bereavement groups that she had the disease because she was sure that it did not affect her ability to facilitate. But the truth was that she was slowing down, not just with her unsteady gait, but mentally as well; she could not seem to think or speak in clear sentences after sunset, as if her cognitive brain worked on solar power.

She glanced at her watch. She had wanted to get there early so that she could have a few minutes with the guest speaker, Henrietta Hooper, a hospital chaplain she had met, of all unlikely places, at the movie theater a few months ago. She started to shuffle so that she could save time. That's what she was now, an official shuffler, because she could no longer pick up her feet when she was in a hurry, could not take the time to watch each step. She could move much faster this way, gliding like an indoor cross-country skier on ballet flats. She had tried walkers, but she kept misjudging the stride, overcompensating, getting her feet caught under the wheels.

She had mastered the art of falling without breaking any bones years ago. She had learned how to land on the soft part of her upper back and lower shoulder, holding her arms close to her sides, always backward. Nobody liked to see an elderly woman fall. Strangers knelt around her, cell phones in hand, ready to dial 911, whispering to each other but shouting questions at her, as if she had fallen down a well and was too far away to hear. She shuffled around the last corner, trying to pick up speed. Maybe Henrietta had already gotten there and would start the meeting without her.

She had left a message for Henrietta to come help her tonight, but she was not sure that Henrietta would be able to come, since the hospital would need extra chaplains on the night call service for all those grisly ER admissions, children who would be hit by cars, choke on candy, and suffocate inside their costumes.

Then she heard someone coming behind her in the hallway, and she turned to look.

"I thought you might need this. You left it in my car the other day. This damn heat is knocking us all off our pins. I tried to use it to scrape that Grim Reaper's head off, but it didn't work. So, here."

Henrietta, dressed formally in a black silk pantsuit, was holding up a cane, light blue, with butterflies, and she slipped it under Ellie's right hand. Then she took her left arm and hooked it through Ellie's, in that charming way Europeans do when strolling down boulevards. It had taken some time for Ellie to get used to this habit of walking as if Henrietta were her own daughter, and now she could not imagine any other way of walking. Suddenly, Ellie felt dizzy and out of balance and she leaned into Henrietta.

"Are you all right, Ellie? Let's stop a minute and let you rest a bit."

Henrietta laid her coat down in the hallway and told Ellie to sit there. Then she went ahead to the conference room to get her some water. Henrietta seemed so much older than her years. She was in her early thirties, she'd told Ellie once, and Ellie did not ask the exact year. Mandy would have turned thirty-two this August.

"You can't possibly understand true suffering until you become a parent," Ellie's younger sister had told her, with a smug hoarseness in her voice that had deepened with the birth of each of her five children, as if she were leaking estrogen out of her throat. Runners must present a certificate of live birth at the registration table before officially entering the Human Race. And Ellie had barely made the qualifiers at forty-five years old, an AMA mother, as it was noted on her medical chart. Not AMA as in Against Medical Advice, because she had become pregnant with a great deal of medical advice, as well as considerable medical intervention. AMA in her case stood for Advanced Maternal Age. She had every prenatal test available at the time, but none of them detected the fatal malformation, the tiny ticking time bomb in the tiny heart. Her baby was already dying before she was born. Was it because the mother was already late before she entered the race?

It had always been hard to keep up with Mandy when they went out trick-or-treating, especially as the night wore on. By late evening, Ellie's body and mind could barely connect with each other. She would weave drunkenly, bumping into people and slurring her words together in a sloppy run-on apology. "So-so-sorry, didn't see you, so-so-sorry." All the other parents, young professionals with double incomes into seven figures, had no time to listen, rushing past her, chasing their little knights and princesses faster and faster, as if none of them could afford to turn down this great deal of first-come, first-served free candy.

She remembered the relief that flowed through her like pure oxygen the moment she waved her flashlight ahead and caught the saving sight of Mandy's orange glow-in-the-dark butterfly wings floating in clear view above the other children's heads. How old was she then? Five? It had been the year that Mandy had suddenly grown into her rich, dark looks.

Mandy had her father's Mediterranean complexion, a head of thick, glossy auburn hair. It fell in cascades of soft ringlet curls around her heart-shaped face, making her look like one of those pageant children whose mother had spent hours with hot rollers and round beauty-salon brushes. She had huge hazel eyes, lush lashes, and rosebud lips that curved upward even when she was not smiling. She woke up looking like a reincarnated silent film actress, her face flushed, full of secrets she could hardly wait to reveal. Mandy's butterfly costume year was also the year that strangers had started reaching out to stroke her head and then catching themselves and stopping, staring in surprise at their own hands in midair. It was disconcerting, her child's siren beauty, a matter of public domain, to be admired from a distance but never directly touched, like fine art in a museum.

What would she look like now? It was cruel timing to take a teenager—the meanest of all tricks from a Trickster God. They would never know how tall she was going to be, whether she would have her mother's compact petite build or her father's long-limbed loping stride or some kind of hybrid all her own. Mandy was frozen in time at her most awkward stage, her breasts swelling, her hips widening, nothing fitting properly, her true size right between the manufactured sizes of the largest girl and the smallest woman. A few days before Mandy died, only a week before her fourteenth birthday, Ellie had taken her shopping for a certain kind of designer jeans.

"I will never get this afternoon of my life back," a father sitting on the floor outside the changing room said to his daughter as she swept by him carrying a pile of denim that must have been worth thousands of dollars. He had set up a portable office there in a half-circle around him, file folder with the months of the year labeled; paper printing calculator; prestamped, preaddressed envelopes. He was paying his bills and shaking his head, defiantly. "I am not going to waste one more moment of it."

He looked ridiculous sitting there, trying to make time obey him even if his surly daughter would not. All of Ellie's friends who were parents had warned her about this time-shift phenomenon, that having a baby would reset her internal clock forever. But it had not happened the way she had imagined. It was Mandy's death, not her birth, that stopped time entirely. None of the moments that happened afterward, even the divorce, registered as moments worth remembering.

Ellie and Henrietta entered the conference room. There was a woman slouching at the far end of the table, with her hands over her eyes as if the light were painful. When she took her hands away, Ellie recognized her immediately, although it had been at least six months since she had come to this group. It was Rachel. The last time she was here, she cheerfully announced that she was done with all the crying, done with sadness, pronounced herself a "grief graduate." Her daughter, Ariel, had died of anorexia a few months earlier. Rachel was dressed tonight in a black turtleneck and black slacks, but she was still shivering, her arms wrapped around her large steel-studded black leather purse, shaped like one of those old-fashioned doctor's bags.

"Hi, Rachel, it's good to see you here," Ellie said as she walked forward, her arms open to enclose her.

"Goddamned Halloween night, I knew this was the one place I could go," Rachel mumbled as she stood up. She was very thin, and Ellie could feel her bones trembling when she hugged her.

Ellie asked Henrietta to light the candle of Hope. It flickered in the draft of the air conditioner but did not go out. Rachel sat down in a seat close to the candle and stretched her hands out in front of it, as if it could warm them like a fire. Ellie looked over her group roster and wondered how many would show up tonight. They tended to arrive in groups, having banded together during the week, going on sad little field trips together, like cemetery visits and run-walk fundraisers for research into childhood diseases, sporting tombstone T-shirts of their dead children's faces and life and death dates stamped across their hearts.

This was the pattern Ellie noticed, although there was not supposed to be a hierarchy of suffering and she discouraged making comparisons about who hurt the most. But natural alliances always seem to form anyway, according to the circumstances of a child's death. There were three distinct subgroups: the mothers who lost children slowly after long illnesses, the mothers who lost children suddenly in accidents, and those who had lost older children to suicide. The mothers of suicide cases usually did not stick around for more than one session because Ellie referred them out to Survivors of Suicide support groups, which had a rolling admission policy and no shortage of applicants.

This is why Rachel was a solo arrival, because anorexia is a grab bag of all three, a slow suicide resulting from a long mental illness, statistically predictable but still shocking in its finality. Rachel was not a good fit for a generalized grief group. Members of the group often shunned mothers whose children had died of seemingly preventable events, like getting into the car with a drunk driver or overdosing on drugs. There was always the unspoken judgment in the air that mothers of anorexics had advance warning and more time to save their children. As if good mothers were supposed to keep their children from starving to death, as if all it took to keep them alive was finding and cooking them more appealing food.

But Rachel would be safe here. This was a more inclusive group, kind to one another, not given to sudden bursts of rage and accusation. Four women came in quietly and took their seats around the oblong conference table. Each one tilted her head solemnly at the flickering candle as if it were on an altar. It was a small gathering, which was just as well for all concerned, considering the timing. Everyone with dead children was spooked tonight.

Last week, they had talked about dreading the coming holidays, with the stores already decked with joy. Ellie confessed that she had sent out holiday cards for fourteen years after Mandy's death, a reverse-life review, so that the last picture sent was Baby's First Christmas, Mandy at four and a half months, toothlessly grinning in a miniature Santa suit. Years later her friends told her how much they dreaded opening her cards each year, and how they could not bear to put them out on display but also could not bear to throw them out. She regretted it now, regretted how so much of her rage was misdirected.

She looked around at the familiar faces, trying to remember details about each one. Then she got to Henrietta. She glowed in this group, with her caramel-colored shoulder length hair, wide-spaced dark blue eyes, and a radiant complexion. She was surrounded by women who had long ago stopped caring about how they looked, prickly thorns around a blooming rose. They came in looking like the people at the homeless shelter where she volunteered. They were wearing the same shapeless sweats they wore to bed, not even noticing the fast-food ketchup stains spattered on their chests and knees.

Rachel was talking now. She did not wait for Ellie to announce check-in.

"And those goddamn skulls everywhere. Reminding me of Ariel, her sunken face, cheekbones so huge and pointy, like they're about to poke through her skin—God—that was so fucked up, those last two years!"

Ellie was alarmed by the raw anger in Rachel's voice. It was as if Ariel had died more recently. What happened to the self-proclaimed grief graduate? Ellie needed to disarm her somehow or she would suck up every second of the two-hour airtime, leaving out all the others. As the group leader, she had to be hypervigilant to the signs of a mother arriving in the midst of immediate crisis. But she couldn't seem to get on top of her own scattershot thoughts tonight, much less follow anyone else's reasoning.

The windowless room had turned stifling hot because the building's air conditioners automatically shut off at six. The stale heat was setting off short circuits in her neurological system so that all her reflexes, mind and body, were moving in slower and slower motion. Clearly, she was on the verge of another major relapse. Profound exhaustion was the proper medical term, and it was the first symptom.

It sounded so romantic, "profound exhaustion," for such a soul-killing feeling. It was impossible to explain to anyone this kind of tired, although the closest analogy could be made to other mothers: the first-trimester overpowering desire to sleep all the time, anywhere, anyplace, as if heavily drugged. She dug her fingernails into her thighs, trying to stay alert. It took every cell in her body to fight the urge to curl up in the corner and go to sleep on the floor. She ground her nails in deeper, her own makeshift bed of nails. Was it time for her to stop doing these groups? Yes, of course it was. She hated herself for being so absorbed in her own needs in the midst of all this seeping, open-wound desperate neediness around her.

Rachel looked around the room, blinking rapidly, as if she were also coming out of a trance. Her eyes were a soft shade of gray, hypnotic, mesmerizing, making it impossible to resist returning the stare. Ellie remembered her story now. Years before Ariel was sick, Rachel had gotten this permanent makeup done, sharp black lines around the edges of her eyelids and lips, with brows dyed to match. Now, tears poured down her smudge-proof, grief-proof face.

Her eyes searched the room as if seeing for the first time that other people were there. She collapsed back into her chair, crumpling in on herself.

Check-in began. Nancy, seventeen-year-old daughter killed in a car crash with her three closest friends when a drunk driver went the wrong way onto their exit ramp. Colleen, son drowned in the neighbor's backyard swimming pool while his parents were preoccupied getting the house ready for his fourth birthday party. Rosalie, six-year-old daughter crushed by a falling tree branch on the kindergarten school playground. Patricia, twelve-year-old son, anaphylactic shock, peanut allergy, ate the wrong candy bar on a sixth-grade field trip.

So the accident group must have carpooled together tonight, escaping any risk of a ringing doorbell and being expected to hand out treats to other people's children. All were single mothers now, as a death in the family almost always killed the marriage as well. This was Rachel's situation. Ellie took a deep breath and pushed the tissue box in front of Rachel, the go-ahead signal that it was her turn to share.

"Ariel's dog is dead. This morning. I should have been ready . . . She's a Maltese mix. Seventeen is old for them. Oh, God, Ariel's age when she . . . Shit."

Rachel reached down to grab her purse, which had fallen off of her lap, and put it back on the table. She opened it and took out a framed photograph of a plump and dimpled toddler holding a fluffy white puppy so tiny it looked like it should come with batteries.

"We got Snowball when Ariel was two," Rachel said. "But the dear little thing was dying so horribly. She had to go. Poor little thing—so sick, kidneys failing, back legs not working, all of it—but . . ."

She spread her hands out on the table, looking down at them, and stopped talking.

"Your last living link to Ariel's life," said Patricia, reaching for the tissue box. "Nobody ever tells you how every other death just keeps opening the door to this one and slamming you in the face with it."

"No more. Not anymore," Rachel said, shaking her head.

She started to root around in her purse again. Patricia slid the tissues back to her, but Rachel ignored the box, intent on finding whatever she was looking for, apparently not tissues. Finally, she pulled something carefully from her purse, bundled in red cloth, and lifted it out with both hands. Ellie's heart lurched. Was it the dead dog? Jesus. It would be small enough to fit in that oversized black coffin of a purse. Calm down and breathe, Ellie told herself. It's probably just another picture. God, she really couldn't do this anymore. She closed her eyes and gripped the arms of her office chair to keep steady. Panic swept over her and she was hyperventilating. Oh, God, she was going to pass out right there in front of everybody.

"Put that down now, Rachel. Help is coming. Five minutes more," Henrietta said, her tone firm and authoritative, as if speaking to a child.

Ellie opened her eyes. Henrietta had dropped her cell phone in Ellie's lap. Ellie looked down at it, a miniature black television screen encased in bright orange plastic with oversize white buttons on the top. It looked like a giant candy corn. Then the screen suddenly lit up and the words CALLING PET scrolled across it, followed by an image of an alarm clock with its minute and hour hands spinning around.

This made no sense to Ellie. Was Henrietta trying to call the dead dog on her cell phone? If she could make that kind of connection then she might as well go the whole distance and call God directly. She was an ordained minister, wasn't she? No, that still didn't make sense. Everything was falling apart and she could not connect the pieces.

Ellie shook her head as if that could clear her view. Maybe it was her vision fading out. She looked down at the cell phone and read it again. CALLING PET. That was exactly what the screen said. And then the clock started to dance, with a smiling happy face where its spinning time hands used to be. Ellie tugged on Henrietta's arm to get her attention. Henrietta's sweater was soft like silk and she couldn't get a grip on it. Henrietta jerked her arm away, and then Ellie realized that it was her skin, not her sweater, she had been pulling on.

"I don't understand. Who is calling? Should I answer?"

But Henrietta was looking at Rachel intently, as if she were the only person in the world who mattered. And Rachel was looking at the swaddled crimson object in her hands. Then she started to unwrap it slowly, knowing everyone was watching her, and smiling to herself, as if this were a party and she were opening up a gift.

"Five minutes, Rachel." Henrietta said. "Look at me and promise me that you will put the gun down for five minutes."

Gun?

"Sure," Rachel said calmly, nodding her head.

She turned the gun over carefully in her hands. It was dull and scratched on the both sides. She did not put it down.

"As soon as I check how many bullets are left. I used one for Snowball this morning."

"No!" Ellie screamed, as she realized finally what was happening. Then she tried to stand up and make a run for the door. How quickly could she get there and get everyone out with her? But she was too slow, and it was so awfully hot, and her feet slid out from under her. The chair caught her as she fell backward, and she was rolling away in the wrong direction, farther and farther from saving herself or anybody else. And then she was being spun around and pushed back to where she started. Nancy had gotten behind her and was wheeling her back to the table, patting her shoulder, as if this happened all the time.

"Rachel. Listen to me. *Right now.*"

Henrietta was not asking anymore. She was demanding.

"Five minutes. Promise me that you won't touch that gun for five minutes."

"All right," Rachel said. She dropped the gun with a thud back on the table.

Nobody said a word as they looked up at the clock and watched the minute hand go around. Seven women. All sitting in a circle around a loaded gun. Nobody seemed to skip a beat. At one point, Nancy shifted her legs restlessly as she stood behind Ellie's chair and sighed. Sighed. Like she was bored. Like five measly minutes was too long to wait for a crazy person to keep a promise. Like there must be more exciting ways to spend five minutes. As if there were nothing important at stake.

And of course, it was true. Even with that suffocating toxic air softening her brain, Ellie could still understand why these women could look at a clock and remain perfectly calm, no matter if there were seven bullets left in that gun, one for each of them. Worse things had already happened than their own deaths.

There were women there who had said so, in this very room over the last year in so many different ways. Some wished they had already died. Others felt as if they were dead already. And others said that they were hoping Heaven existed only so that they could die as soon as possible to see their children once again. At some point Ellie had asked each of these women if they had a particular plan, and they shrugged. One of them said (was it Patricia?) that she could not even make a plan to program the coffee maker, much less a plan to kill herself. It took too much energy. Yes. It took Rachel six months to get the strength to come up with the plan. And one dead dog.

There was a pounding at the door. And the sounds of male voices, and the squawking of police radios. The door burst open and four uniformed men, two in blue, two in white, walked in, and with them the most wonderfully cool breeze, washing over all of them. And Ellie's brain cloud cleared. Now she understood. PET. Psychological Emergency Team.

PET moved like a splendidly choreographed dance. The first man who came in went straight for the gun and disappeared with it. The second two men gently escorted Rachel, arm in arm, out the door, out of the room, and then out of the building into a waiting ambulance, not stopping or slowing down for one moment. The fourth man led the group outside so that they could take full deep gulps of the brisk night air.

That's when the PET medic told them that Rachel was being placed under a three-day hold in a locked ward of a nearby hospital. There was nothing more any of them could do right now. The group left without another word, some still holding tissues against their eyes, absorbing the hopelessness of the night's events.

Ellie and Henrietta stayed behind, sat down on the front steps, and huddled together. They talked briefly about when they had last spent time together in a parking lot with ambulances and police officers and waving good-bye to another lost soul.

"We should not make a habit of this kind of thing," Henrietta said, leaning back against the Grim Reaper's shadow.

The Viewing Room NOVEMBER

Almost all major faith traditions have easily accommodated the secular holiday of Thanksgiving. Yet the everyday practice of giving thanks for one's blessings requires concerted effort. Gratitude, like compassion, is a difficult exercise in spiritual discipline, growing in power only when practiced steadily and deliberately over the years. Children must be reminded over and over to say *thank you* and *I am sorry*, memorized like simple prayers or chants, so that the timing becomes reflexive. The ultimate enlightened being offers appreciation before the gift is opened, and sorrow for the pain before knowing its cause. Then the giver becomes more important than the gift and the wounded more important than the wound.

The viewing room inflates compassion so that it flutters constantly above the stillness of life giving great wings to that thing with feathers called hope. But it suffocates gratitude like paper over rock, taking one's breath away for expressing appreciation so soon after both the gift and the giver have disappeared. There are no blessings to be found here, disguised (and why, on earth, should blessings need to be disguised?) or undisguised. The hospital chaplains know better than to try any kind of spiritual damage control. There are no cushiony words, sweet scents, or comforting rituals that can buffer the pain of viewing a loved one's body, freshly dead. This room narrows to a terrifying, airless, pitch-black hallway even to the ones who truly believe that it is a journey from one life to the next. Every living soul must shrink down to its crawl-through size in order to survive a moment here.

Later, in a more formal setting, the body safely out of sight, the priests, ministers, rabbis, imams, and even well-intentioned friends will attempt to wash away despair with their own cleansing word potions. They will urge the mourners to choose celebrating the life over grieving the death—as if this were easy, as if this were some tiny hop in a two-step dance and not a heart-splitting fall from grace. It takes superhuman strength to return to living after losing the life we have loved above and beyond our own. It requires gratitude weighted down so heavily with accumulated blessings that it pulls us back to earth, determined to keep deserving them.

[PASSERBY]

Some people view life as a gift, and some people view life as an entitlement. But Ellie knew she was different. She viewed life as a short-term bridge loan, and she was always behind on the payments. She was aware that at any moment the collateral could be repossessed. When anything bad happened to her, she asked not *why me* but *why not me*. She wondered if this was the beginning of the end that she had expected even earlier. She knew firsthand that sight is an anticipatory sense, its greatest value resting in the warning of danger coming straight toward her. She knew this because she had lost her vision for an extended period of time, enough time to live the rest of her life, once recovered, with one foot in the blind world and one foot in the sighted world, teetering between, never sure where both feet would end up, like a person who can't swim must feel stepping down from a dock into a boat, unsteady, rocking back and forth, legs growing wider apart, until finally a choice must be made.

Ellie had fallen many times before, but she knew that this was the last time. It was dark ahead, but she walked toward it anyway, feeling certain that a light would emerge to guide her steps, motion-detector lights like the ones she had installed around her house. She took the stairway that she thought was leading to a parking garage, pleased that she would get to her car before the other people leaving the theater, who were still waiting for elevators. She took that first air-step and knew immediately. There were no stairs, and there would be no soft landing. Here it was, the abrupt ending, and she relaxed into the fall, grateful to be reclaimed at last.

She was not afraid of death. She knew many people said that they were not afraid of death, just of suffering beforehand, but in her former days as a hospice nurse she had seen how people clung to life, wracked with ferocious, unrelenting pain, confessing in a whisper, *I am so afraid, so afraid.* But her worst suffering had already happened, when Mandy, her only child, died, taking the poisonous sting out of her own death. The other mothers in her bereavement group had said the nights would be the hardest, but that was not true. She welcomed the setting of the sun, making her feel as if it were practically normal to crawl back into the waiting, unmade bed. No, it was the mornings that were excruciating, waking up into one more day without her daughter, needing every bit of emotional strength to move her eyelids open.

"Eleanor, can you hear me. Can you tell me where you are? Eleanor! Eleanor!"

A strong male voice of increasing urgency and brisk impatience. This man's voice was entirely different from the two voices she had heard a few minutes before. After she fell, a husky older voice, not asking questions, but talking to her, "Oh, my, you've done it now. Poor thing, you can't get up from this," and then later more questions, a young, breathless voice, "Where does it hurt, squeeze my hand if you can hear me and show me where it hurts. Blink if you understand me." And she had tried to blink but her body, every piece of her body, was disconnected from her mind. And now this voice, a doctor's voice, and she knew that this man was highly educated and was irritated with her, or with the nurses around her.

Now she wanted to open her eyes and answer the orientation questions, the who, what, where, and when of the moment, oriented to person, situation, place, and time, but she had nothing left. She had asked these questions of people herself, trying to gauge the flimsiness of their grasp upon the solid world. She wanted to answer him because she was not in any kind of pain or discomfort and she wanted to reassure the voice that everything was all right. And she wanted to tell him to call her Ellie, not the formal name on her driver's license.

"Unresponsive," he said, in a quieter, resigned voice, to someone who was taking notes. "Severe head trauma, probable skull fracture, massive bleeding from lacerations, need a head and neck CT stat if she makes it that long."

Well, none of that sounded very encouraging. But the good news was that she must be breathing or they would be forcing a tube down her throat. The brutality of the emergency room had always disturbed her, and she had left instructions about what procedures she would allow at the end to prolong her life. Damn few, actually. But the directive was locked in her glove compartment. Did she drive here? She could not remember a car or an ambulance. No, she flew here! And she was getting ready to fly again, up through the ceiling, up past the clouds, flying away, far away from the voice, drifting into a deep silence that swaddled her, arms and legs folding in, now certain that she never had to move by herself again. It would all happen without her trying. And she was too exhausted from all the trying to turn back, anyway.

Henrietta had been dreading this moment ever since she took the hospital chaplaincy position. She had hoped it would never happen. But now that moment was here. She was paged to the viewing room and the dead patient was not a stranger but someone she knew and loved.

She had reviewed the ER notes over and over, sobbing at her computer in the Spiritual Care Office. She wished someone else could read it with her and help her understand how this had happened. But she was the only chaplain on call. Apparently, Ellie had fallen from a forty-foot height and landed crumpled against the partial concrete wall of the construction site, a new parking structure for the theater. Her head had been pierced—oh, God, pierced—by a rebar. And worst of all, she did not die right away. Poor Ellie, poor dear, sweet Ellie. Why would she be walking there, in the dark, so late and alone? Was her MS in relapse, and was she walking with a cane and lost her balance? But that would not explain why the paramedics had told the doctor that she must have torn down the thick yellow caution tape and then carefully squeezed herself through the opening between the locked fence gates to tumble to her death.

Unless this was what Ellie wanted.

They had talked about suicide, more than once, actually. Ellie had asked Henrietta if she had ever contemplated taking her own life. Henrietta had answered quickly, and now she realized probably too smugly, "I would never give back the gift," sounding as if she believed that suicide was an act of weakness, a fatal character flaw, an unforgivable failure to appreciate life. Ellie had not seemed offended by the remark, but it had effectively ended the conversation until later, until necessity demanded that they revisit the subject in the most painfully direct way.

It was Halloween night, almost a month ago, and Henrietta had attended a mothers' bereavement group, one that Ellie had been leading for years. A disturbed woman had pulled out a gun and threatened to kill herself. Henrietta, a practiced crisis interventionist, had managed to call for help just in time. She was concerned about what Ellie had said to her later.

But that was not what bothered Henrietta the most about that night, now that she looked back on it through the lens of this terrible possibility. It was not the things Ellie did not do or say that night but what she did say to Henrietta later, after Rachel had been put on psychiatric hold, after the rest of the group had been counseled and escorted home. She had said that if she had been alone in the room with Rachel, with no witnesses, she doubted she would have stopped her. And she might have asked her to kill her first.

How louder a cry for help could there be than that? Yet Henrietta had let that statement sit there between them without comment, mistakenly thinking that if she silently listened to her friend's true feelings, she would never act upon them once they were let out into the night air. That it would all disappear like a harmless ghost, as if there had ever been such a thing. Ghosts always haunt somebody for a reason, usually to tell them something important. Well, Henrietta had missed that message.

But so many people loved Ellie. Didn't she know that? All those mothers who had leaned on her strength, all those dying hospice patients who borrowed her deep faith, desperate people who counted on her to see them through the darkest time of their lives. And she had done that so well that one of them had called to ask for a viewing at two o'clock in the morning, only a few hours after Ellie's death. The nurses who prepared Ellie's body had also known her and had taken greater care with her, wrapping her in layers of freshly laundered and warmly dry hospital gowns, as if she could still catch a chill.

Henrietta stood by the gurney in the viewing room and hesitated for a moment before sliding her hands into the black vinyl bag that covered Ellie from the neck down and pressing a rosary into the folds of cloth, close to where she thought Ellie's hands would be. She was careful not to touch her skin even though she wanted to change the bandage on the left side of her head, which was no longer bleeding but still had yellow antiseptic stains weeping through. Ellie was a coroner's case since the accident was still under investigation, and nobody could touch the body directly until the Medical Examiner's officials came. Were they even thinking homicide now? Could it be true that somebody had pushed her, that anybody would want to kill her?

There was a knock at the door that made Henrietta jump. She looked up to see a tall, elderly man walk through the door. He was African American, quite thin, wearing a thick down coat that was caked with mud at the edges. He stood at the back of the room, and Henrietta went over to him.

"Do you want to come closer to say good-bye?"

He shook his head and backed away a few steps but did not turn around to leave. He was shaking as if he were scared she was going to rise up and go after him. He looked at the body from a safe distance. Then he reached up and took the black wool cap off of his head and held it to his chest, closing his eyes.

"Would you like to pray with me?" Henrietta asked.

He blinked at her and then narrowed his eyes to inspect her hospital ID badge.

"No, thanks. I just came to pay my respects is all."

He put his hat back on and turned to leave, but Henrietta called out to him.

"Did you know Ellie long?"

She avoided asking the more obvious and interesting question about how he knew Ellie. And then she remembered that Ellie volunteered at a homeless shelter several afternoons a week. This must be one of her—clients? No, she called them something else. Guests. As if they were guests in her own home and she were hostess for parties every day.

"No, I never met her," he said quietly. "Not until tonight."

"You saw her fall," Henrietta said.

She knew it. She could tell by his expression that he had seen Ellie die. She knew exactly how that kind of guilt wore on a face. She had seen it her first night as a chaplain, in this room, when a father came to see his infant son, whom he had shaken and thrown against a wall.

"Yes, and I'm so sorry," he said, looking at her with tears in his eyes, confirming her fears.

She knew he was about to confess, and she wanted to stop him, to make him wait until somebody else, anybody else but a minister, came into the room to hear him out. There were rules about this kind of conversation. The boundaries were set clearly in the case law. Confessions of a crime already committed are protected by priest-penitent privilege. Only a clear intention of causing harm in the future waived the privilege.

But what about God's law? Why wasn't she held to that law, the law she had promised to obey above all others? Why couldn't she hold this murderer accountable, at least here, at least now, when she could drag him over there and make him look closely at the damage? She would start by showing him the thick dried blood that streaked and flattened Ellie's silver hair against her cheeks, hideous dark-red earmuffs.

"What did you do?"

At least she could hear the details, hope that it was fast and he had not hurt Ellie before he pushed her.

"I took down the tape. Like I do every night. It's where I keep my roll. I slide down into there, and I get some sleep where nobody can bother me. I take the tape off, but then I always put it back up before the workers come back. I never thought anybody would come there at night. I never told nobody where I keep my roll."

"Roll?"

He sighed. "My sleep roll. I found that place two months ago, just as it started to get cold. It's warm down in that hole. And I was safe from the cops, from the security guards kicking me awake."

"You were sleeping there?"

"Yes, I was asleep but then I heard her cry out, and I looked up, and there she was coming down. She landed against the wall and there was this metal—"

"No, don't!" Henrietta interrupted him. "Enough! If you pushed her, if you did something to her, just tell the truth. To me. In here. In God's name, tell me the truth!"

He stared at her and then slapped his hands together, holding them up, mock prayer, in front of her face. She flinched and held her breath.

"You calling me a killer? I'm homeless, Lady Minister, but not brainless. I wouldn't kill a person and then show up here later."

He was right, of course. Why had she been so quick to accuse and judge? And now she throbbed with regret, endless, irreparable regret over words said or unsaid and things done or never done, the same regret that she used to try to assuage when a visitor expressed it. Always remembering the last scenes, the last words. If only I had said this or if only I had done that. And now it was her turn.

"I am so sorry. She was my friend. I am trying to understand why this happened."

"I am sorry for your loss then, Ma'am," he said.

"Why are you here to see her, if you never knew her?" Why would a stranger ever come into the viewing room to see a stranger?

"They dragged me in—the paramedics. It was her blood on me, not my own, but they wouldn't listen and made me get checked out."

Henrietta could now see that it was not mud on his jacket, and she had to look away.

"I tried to stop the bleeding, and I couldn't. And then I went up and got help. It was the last thing I wanted to do, let me tell you, to let them know where I was, but I thought I had to do it. Somebody had to do it. I thought about running, and I don't know why, but I didn't want to leave her there alone, so I pointed my flashlight up and swooped it back and forth. They saw it."

She looked at him closely now and saw that he had bloodstains on the arms of his jacket and across his chest. Had he held Ellie as she lay dying, at least, so she knew somebody was there, somebody cared?

"I don't know. I just wanted to see her one more time, in the light. I saw her fall, like you figured. Only witness. They called me a Passerby in that report. But I didn't."

"Didn't what?"

"Didn't pass her by."

He smiled at her then, and she saw him clearly. His upper front teeth were missing, so it was a child's smile in an old face.

"Is there a word for that? Stayingby? Should be a word for that, 'cause I seem to be stuck here staying by. I'll be honest. I don't think all of her has left us quite yet."

She looked at him, and his eyes were bright. He was afraid. But not of the body, and not of what he had done, but of something that would not let go, had not left this room, and she felt it too. How to release it?

She smiled back at him. "There is a word for it. For you. For what you did."

"What?" he asked.

"Angel," she answered.

He shook his head, scowling. "No, don't be saying that! Don't be thinking that I'm some kind of saint in dirty clothes or prophet just because I'm on the streets. Don't be thinking that by being nice to me, you will get your own halo polished up with a poor soul's gratefulness."

He must have given that speech before. It packed a hard punch. Henrietta had never had anybody speak to her this way. She had people in here mad at other people, mad at God, but this was the first time somebody was genuinely mad at her. It was a stupid thing to say. As if she decided who the angels were in the world.

"I'm sorry. I was trying to give you a compliment, to praise you for . . ."

"For doing the right thing? Save it. You don't have to believe in God or angels to know what's right."

Henrietta held out her hand. "Let me start over. My name is Henrietta, and that lady over there is Ellie."

He gave her a gummy grin, and touched her hand briefly. "Name's Leo, not Passerby."

"Well, Leo, we are all just passing through, aren't we?" Henrietta said.

"And some of us just can't ever stop moving, that's for sure."

"Ellie worked with the homeless. She went down to a shelter and volunteered every day since her daughter died."

"Well, at least she wasn't one of those do-gooders who show up only on Thanksgiving when the news cameras are out."

"No, she loved the work. She said that after Mandy died, she could not stop making her lunch every day, and so she put it in the car and handed it out to the first needy person she saw. And then she just wanted to help more and more people."

"Yep, plenty of them in this city, that's for sure."

"It's the warm weather," Henrietta said.

Leo smirked. "Damn, I'm tired of hearing that. It's not the warm weather, or Florida would have more of us. It's the cold-hearted people sealed in their cars, not seeing anything but the road ahead."

"Ellie was not one of those people, Leo. She had a tough life, a lot of losses. She always had a roof over her head, but she said she knew what it was like to lose your place in the world."

"Yeah, your kid dying on you will do that. My life turned to shit after my boy was killed. Drinking was the only way I could see fit to breathe. And even so, it was hard to breathe for the longest time. The air had knife blades in it."

"I'm sorry," Henrietta said.

"Don't be sorry for something you had nothing to do with, Preacher-Lady."

He was a prickly character. She did not know how to talk to him.

"Leo. Is there anything I can do for you?"

He seemed startled by the question. Then he walked over to Ellie again and stood by the gurney. Henrietta went over to stand beside him.

"I think it was part of God's plan to take her now. I really do," Henrietta said quietly.

Leo flinched. "You know what I think? I think we say death is only part of God's plan when we agree with the timing, that's what I think. So you must have thought this was a good time for her to die."

"No, I didn't mean that! I did not want her to die. I loved her."

"Well, then, tell me something. How come you know God's plan? What makes you so special you can speak for God? Explain why He does what He does. No disrespect, but I just wanna know."

Henrietta bowed her head, ashamed at the turn the conversation was taking. This man was asking an impossible question. She did not know God's plan any more than anybody else, but in her religion, ministers mediated for God, were expected to explain away the inconsistencies and attribute it to mystery. Yet, how could death always be part of a plan, when babies died of brain cancer or were burned alive by their parents? After almost a year in this hospital, the place she had come to renew her faith, she had come instead to the terrible conclusion that she did not believe in a loving New Testament God but the Old Testament punishing God. This changed the whole picture, not necessarily for the better. But Leo was waiting for her answer.

"Tell me about your son," she said, trying to distract him. "I know that losing a child is the worst thing that a parent has to bear."

He shook his head and sighed. "No, it is not the worst. The worst is having a child die and it's your fault."

Oh, God. This was a mistake. So this is how the guilt on his face came about. And her heart lurched because she knew her legal obligation. The rules again. Any criminal act regarding a child was an exception to the confidentiality privilege. But Henrietta did not want to hear another sad dead child story. She had only the capacity to grieve for Ellie, and not a drop more left. She closed her eyes, and only then did she feel it. A draft of cool air against her face, in a room with a closed door and no windows. She felt her hair gently smoothed back. Ellie. She always called her Cool Breeze. Ellie. She would have forgiven him.

She opened her eyes.

He sighed. "She's completely gone now," he said.

"Yes," Henrietta agreed. "She's gone."

And she took a long last look at her friend. A few seconds later, when she looked back to Leo, he was also gone.

Leo knew how to disappear from view in a matter of seconds. Those seconds between the shout of a cop and the pounding of his stick. Those seconds between a scared woman walking her dog and the spray of pepper in his face. He always had an exit strategy. He had to get out of there, that viewing room. He had to run, even before he could tell the woman in there something that might have eased her pain.

He would have told her about what he saw when he shined a flashlight in her friend's face. A look of beautiful peace, even with that metal sticking into her brain. She was still breathing, but she never opened her eyes. Yet there was not a bit of hurt in her face or in her body, no flailing arms and legs. He had seen people die on the streets many times, and they always fought it. Sidewalk surfers going for another thrill ride and panicking when they realized it was their last. This was what he needed to see back at the hospital one more time, the comfort of that sweet face. Then the air moving through the room just confirmed it. She must be one of the good ones. Not like him. Heaven had a place for her.

Her friend said the dead woman had lost a daughter, and that she had lost her place in the world. How did she find her way back? Or was she still lost until now? Well, now she was finally home. Could it be suicide? He heard the nurses talking about it just three curtains away. He sure got that. How many times had he tried to end his life and failed to do that right, like most things? But he had done right by her. When he saw the body fall toward him, he had woken from a dream about his son. Maybe her scream woke him, but it wasn't loud, more like a squeak, the way people do when they are startled, the way those damn taggers did when he used to sleep underneath the bridge, and he started to move. Like they were not really scared. As if a body moving in the dark was just another twist to the night's adventure, dipping their tiny toes into the criminal life.

He remembered her body flying down toward him and landing hard against the concrete. He held her as he had never been able to hold his three-year-old son who had fallen from a window while his crackhead daddy was screwing a strawberry. Lady of Leisure, she called herself, and her leisure was exchanging the use of her body for more drugs to numb it. He had not heard his boy fall, but only heard the ambulance sirens. It was already too late. That's how come he knew about hospital viewing rooms. His boy did not have any nice calm look on his messed-up little face. His mother tried to rip Leo apart with nail scissors in that room, but he didn't feel the cuts. Was it the drugs? No. Long after the shit was out of his system, he still felt nothing, not even the cold pavement beneath his head every night.

But earlier tonight he had felt everything. He was hurting all over, absorbing pain deep into his bones. He felt the awful hole in her head, the broken neck, the shattered ribs. Was this God's punishment? To make him feel what he had not been able to feel before? Leo believed in a vindictive God, or at least some kind of harsh disciplinary one, like his father, always sharpening his belt, keeping it ready. He still believed that God was a giant whipping hand, waiting for him to do the worst thing. Yes, the worst thing. Had he surprised God when he chose to call for help, even though that exposed him and his hiding place?

He needed a hit, really bad. But he could not go back there to get his stuff. Crime scene now. And he was the criminal, simply for having no place else to go. Even the paramedics had searched him roughly, not looking for wounds, but looking for anything he might have stolen from her. That's really why they brought him in—not to clean him up like they said, but to check his pockets.

The hurting began when he got to the hospital. The nurses had no sooner laid him out in that hospital bed, covered in blankets, when he started to bawl like a baby. He had never hurt this bad, like his legs were being scattershot, like hot pokers through his knees. This was the first time he had been able to stretch his legs out and rest them for seven years. The muscles were spastic, trying to jump out of his skin. It was like coming inside from the cold, back in Detroit where he grew up, after his hands were frostbitten. He had not felt his fingers when they were freezing, but the thawing out sure smacked him down good.

He wondered what was on the other side of thawing out, after the freezing and unfreezing of your heart. Would it be that kind of peace he saw on her face at the end? Had she finally seen some way clear of all the pain and was giving in, sinking into it? Would God forgive him enough to let him have that at the end? He would lean his life toward earning that grace now. He could try. He owed it to his boy to try to make it back home to see him again. He still had time left to try.

The Viewing Room DECEMBER

What is the right way to face the end of life? Some ways appear more courageous, more efficient, or simply not as gruesome as some others. But could there possibly be a perfect way to die? And if so, why does it matter?

In most cases, the circumstances of our death will not be within our control, no matter how carefully we write the end-of-life instructions, research the options, and counsel our loved ones about what medical procedures are acceptable. Ultimately, people tend to die in the same way they have lived—the best way possible until they are forced to stop.

Still, the specter of Christmas Future haunts us. We shudder at the image of being dragged out into the night, ordered to look upon our own graves from a chilling distance, the big reveal of the dreaded number, that final date cast so finally in stone. But are we focusing our vision on the wrong spot, on the birth and death dates, and not on the dash in between? And when we examine that dash, we must try to see that its length does not have any effect on its depth, the dash now an imprint left forever in our hearts and minds and souls.

[SAFE SURRENDER]

"We've got to stop meeting like this, you know," Maurice said, as soon as he saw Henrietta coming down the hospital hallway.

She frowned at him.

"Are you the on-call tonight?" she asked.

"No," he said. "Got an urgent text on my cell to meet someone here. So, I figured the on-call must have bailed."

"Me, too," she said. "I stopped signing up for the night shift a few weeks ago. My year rotation is almost up. Can you believe that? But it looked to me like this was some kind of emergency."

It was close to midnight on Christmas Eve.

Henrietta peered at the one door in the basement hallway that was not decorated for Christmas. She gasped when she saw that the coded lock was missing. The viewing room was never left unlocked, and only Spiritual Care and Janitorial Services had the code, changed weekly, due to the awkward time two nurses were caught doing more than just looking at bodies.

They both heard it before they saw it. A kittenlike whimpering. They stared at each other, motionless. The sound stunned them, two hospital chaplains who were not easily stunned, thinking there was nothing about death that they had not seen already within the walls of this room. It can't be what it sounds like, but it can't be anything else.

And then, they moved together, quickly, across the room, toward the sound of life. Yes, the sound of life!

It was coming from the tiny body shaking on the gurney, swaddled to the neck in white, struggling to get its limbs free of its confinement. Maurice was the first to touch the baby. He gently rolled down the material, soft white cotton, several T-shirts tied together, instead of the usual white vinyl body bag. He freed the baby's arms first so he could examine the hospital bracelet around the tiny wrist.

"No name," he said, turning toward Henrietta. "No shame, no blame, no names."

Those words were posted in gigantic red letters on the Emergency Room entrance doors, the slogan of the Safe Surrender Laws. The anonymous mother who gave up her baby within seventy-two hours of birth would not be prosecuted for abandonment, and the bracelet had no identification and therefore no way to trace.

"But how did the baby end up *here*, for God's sake?" Henrietta asked.

"Really! Of all the gin joints in the world," Maurice said, laughing softly.

"You have got to stop talking in old movie clichés," Henrietta said.

Maurice raised his eyebrows at her. "Really? Here we are on Christmas Eve or Christmas Day, for Christ's sake, with a newborn baby in the unlikeliest of places, and you think I can talk any other way?"

It was true. Nobody—*no live body*—would ever end up in the viewing room by mistake. This was a place for the living to look upon the dead one last time. The viewing room was a stage carefully set for last acts of human drama—for graceful exits, not grand entrances.

"I can't do this anymore," Henrietta said.

"Oh, you poor, precious thing," Maurice said. But he was not talking to her. He was talking to the baby, swaying it back and forth in his arms. "You have landed in the worst place with the worst people in this hospital when it comes to handling a baby. Terrible luck. Poor dear."

It was true. Both of them were better prepared for endings than beginnings. They had become close friends at the hospital during their work on the late-night shift helping people face the darkest moments of their lives. Each one lived alone, without a partner, without children, and although they were both ministers, neither had enough faith to run a church full of believers. This was a dirty secret they shared, separate from the other chaplains in the office.

Henrietta had lost her faith in God, or at least an interventionist God, on the day her brother was killed in a car accident. He bled to death while the ambulance on its way to him crashed and took two more lives. She had started a chaplaincy rotation in hopes that she could find that faith in the very place she lost it.

Maurice was the veteran, twelve years as a chaplain. He had not lost his faith in God, but he had lost all faith in the underlying goodness of his fellow humans. This happened on the day of his mother's murder. He always signed up for the night shift because he liked being with people who were comfortable, even companionable, in the hours when the rest of the world was asleep. Like moles or bats, some creatures have eyes that can see better in the dark and can brighten the blackest corner of the cave for the other creatures crouching there. Maurice and Henrietta knew a lot about waiting in dank, dark corners for the light to arrive.

They had found their calling as they shared this sad fellowship, their own church of nonstop grieving, doors always open, the hospital guaranteeing them a large flock of the spiritually wounded. There was only one sermon they could preach, particularly when the viewing room was the pulpit. *Keep breathing and keep moving.* "You may have to walk through the valley of the shadow," Maurice always said, "but for God's sake, you don't have to set up camp and live there." Every night they worked hard to dissolve the paralytic spell death cast over those left behind. It was a different kind of pastoral care, the job of moving the living in and out of this room before the sight of death froze them forever.

The baby whimpered again, its face now flushed and scrunched up.

"We need to return her," Maurice said as he gave the fussing baby to Henrietta to hold.

"Let's just keep him for a few more minutes, first," Henrietta said, putting the baby against her right shoulder, the downy head warm against her neck.

"Which is it—a *her* or a *him?*" Maurice asked, his eyebrows, raised in mock horror at their confusion.

They laughed at themselves, knowing their reasons for projecting personal gender preferences and also knowing that none of those reasons mattered.

Maurice took the child into his arms again, and the cries subsided.

He looked at Henrietta and held up his hand to stop her question before it began. "No, I never wanted to have one of my own," he said. "But I love borrowing one, whenever I can, just for a moment, just to recharge. I do that every chance I get. I don't leave this hospital from the basement floor after my shift, I go up first to the ninth floor, birth and delivery, and try to get some kind of spiritual palate cleansing."

He took a deep breath and closed his eyes in ecstasy.

"Really? All these months together, and you never told me that?" Henrietta was intrigued. They had shared so much about their personal theologies, doubts, crises of faith, and he had never told her that he had found a decompression chamber better than her Manhattan Beach Mommy movies.

He held the baby closer. "I don't know how anybody can breathe in the smell of a newborn baby and not believe in *something.*"

"If that's really true," Henrietta said, her arms uplifted, "then you have to share. Please."

The last time she had held a baby had been in this room nine months ago, in April. Henrietta had watched a teenage boy sob over the body of a baby he had shaken to death. But this was not the most shocking revelation of that night for Henrietta. It was the fact that she could not pray—not for the baby, not for the mother, not even for her wretched, resentful self. It was the hospital security guard who knelt with the handcuffed murderer. She had stared helplessly at their bowed heads from above, feeling nothing.

But holding this baby right now, this living, breathing baby, melted her. She nodded at Maurice and inhaled deeply.

"I can't come back here again," she said, blinking through the tears. "Every time I look at that gurney, I see the faces of every person I've seen before. Like some vile, floating holograph of bodies, shimmering above the one that just arrived. It's awful, it's—"

"Time to go," Maurice said. "When you're done, you're done."

"When you're done, you're done," Henrietta repeated softly. She looked at Maurice. "Tell me. Honestly. Just between us. Do you believe in all that?"

Maurice looked confused. "What? In burnout, or compassion fatigue, or whatever they call it now? Sure. Seen it all the time. Eventually we all will go bat-shit crazy when we start seeing more dead people than living people. Yes, I do believe in that."

"No," Henrietta sighed. "I mean the idea that some part of us is never completely done. In some form or another—it keeps going. I think I have felt that here."

Maurice smiled at her. "Well, I do believe that. I believe we will all come together again." He let the baby close its tiny fist around his finger. "That will be the true test of our faith, honey. That will be the Christian Olympic Gold Medal event of Forgiveness. If God forgives all souls, then I have to sit for eternity with the man who killed my mother. I hope it's not anytime too soon because I am not ready."

"Are any of us ready, Maurice? Ever see anybody in this room let go easily? They come here because they are never ready to let go."

"That's why I can still show up here. For me, it's not about seeing death in this room. It's the opposite. It's the most life-affirming work that I can do."

Henrietta shifted the child to her other shoulder so she could see Maurice's face, see if he was truly listening as a friend and not as a chaplain.

"But I just can't handle the children dying anymore. I just can't. I have seen my last one die here. I must make sure of that. Or I will fall off the edge of the world."

She told him Molly's story.

Molly was the little girl she had been visiting in the Pediatric Hospice ward. Two words that should never be put in the same sentence, much less have a dedicated wing. Pediatric Hospice.

Molly was dying of a particularly vicious form of leukemia, had tried and failed every treatment, was fading away, inch by inch on her underdeveloped ten-year-old frame. She had been in the hospital for so long that she felt more comfortable there than at home, where her single working mother cared for three younger sisters.

Molly knew it would be better for everybody if she just stayed there, where there was always somebody to listen to her. Molly loved to talk. But what she really wanted most of all, she told Henrietta, was more than the hospital staff's attention. She wished that every person she had ever loved, ever known even, would be cuddled up in sleeping bags outside her door. And then she could go out anytime she wanted, anytime a memory overtook her and she couldn't sleep. She would look at all the sleeping bags, and wake one of them up, and say, "Remember this?"

Molly was the only patient who had asked Henrietta for her number. Not her cell phone number, but a number far more privately guarded. The exact number of people she had watched die. And Henrietta had not hesitated. Sixty-three. And before Molly could ask the next question, she answered it. Sixteen were children.

Molly was reassured by this fact somehow, in a way that Henrietta had never thought such a number would reassure anyone. Then, late one night last week, her last official on-call assignment, a nurse on the unit had paged her to Molly's bed. Molly was crying uncontrollably. She would not talk about it with anyone but Henrietta. When the antianxiety drugs had finally calmed her, she told Henrietta that she was thinking about the dying thing. Molly was grieving her own death.

Other chaplains would have said a prayer at this time, but Henrietta was still not talking to God, and particularly right then, in those hellish circumstances. She tried whenever she could to help patients build their own faith out of their own experiences. But ten years old?

So she talked about how time had so many different speeds and forms and about how it was stretchable, like the biggest rubber band. This was a conversation that often happened in this unit. The Pediatric Hospice kids hated time—real time anyway. Their rooms had no clocks or calendars pinned up to the bulletin boards.

Henrietta remembered that Molly had been put under general anesthetic for many procedures. So they talked about that, how she had closed her eyes just before surgery and then opened them when it was done. How strange and magical that it was one half a second to her and three hours to the doctors and nurses and her family, three hours on the clock that felt like days, waiting, afraid and waiting.

"Maybe it is like that," Molly said. "I close my eyes here and open them up there. I'll see everybody already there with me, everybody, we will all be on the same time, God's time, and it will all work out." She clung to that belief that her dying wouldn't hurt anybody. In the closing and opening of her eyes, an ending and a beginning. Molly died a few hours later. Number 64.

Both Maurice and Henrietta were crying now, as she finished the story. And then the baby started crying.

"We have to give her up," Henrietta said. "She's hungry and wet, and needs to be on her way to finding some kind of home, somehow."

It was the baby's next chapter that they were considering. It did not matter anymore how the child arrived in the viewing room, only how it would leave. But if they had to propose a theory, Maurice thought it was the child of one of the hospital cleaning staff, or a relative or friend of one. Henrietta thought that Maurice had borrowed the baby from another unit, setting her up, loaning out his faith as a parting gift to her. And the motion-sensor cameras had been taken away, like the door's coded lock. So the mystery of the infant's provenance was never solved.

Henrietta wiped the tears from her face with the baby's T-shirt as she followed Maurice out the door to take the baby upstairs.

Maurice stopped and turned around.

"Hey, there," he said, reaching out to caress her face, rubbing his thumbs gently at the corners of her eyes, the palms of his hands warming her cheeks.

"You will leave here and you will be fine. But remember this. You will be all right if you remember this."

THE FLANNERY O'CONNOR AWARD
FOR SHORT FICTION

DAVID WALTON **EVENING OUT**

LEIGH ALLISON WILSON **FROM THE BOTTOM UP**

SANDRA THOMPSON **CLOSE-UPS**

SUSAN NEVILLE **THE INVENTION OF FLIGHT**

MARY HOOD **HOW FAR SHE WENT**

FRANÇOIS CAMOIN **WHY MEN ARE AFRAID OF WOMEN**

MOLLY GILES **ROUGH TRANSLATIONS**

DANIEL CURLEY **LIVING WITH SNAKES**

PETER MEINKE **THE PIANO TUNER**

TONY ARDIZZONE **THE EVENING NEWS**

SALVATORE LA PUMA **THE BOYS OF BENSONHURST**

MELISSA PRITCHARD **SPIRIT SEIZURES**

PHILIP F. DEAVER **SILENT RETREATS**

GAIL GALLOWAY ADAMS **THE PURCHASE OF ORDER**

CAROLE L. GLICKFELD **USEFUL GIFTS**

ANTONYA NELSON **THE EXPENDABLES**

NANCY ZAFRIS **THE PEOPLE I KNOW**

DEBRA MONROE **THE SOURCE OF TROUBLE**

ROBERT H. ABEL **GHOST TRAPS**

T. M. MCNALLY **LOW FLYING AIRCRAFT**

ALFRED DEPEW **THE MELANCHOLY OF DEPARTURE**

DENNIS HATHAWAY **THE CONSEQUENCES OF DESIRE**

RITA CIRESI **MOTHER ROCKET**

DIANNE NELSON **A BRIEF HISTORY OF MALE NUDES IN AMERICA**

CHRISTOPHER MCILROY **ALL MY RELATIONS**

ALYCE MILLER **THE NATURE OF LONGING**

CAROL LEE LORENZO **NERVOUS DANCER**

C. M. MAYO **SKY OVER EL NIDO**

WENDY BRENNER **LARGE ANIMALS IN EVERYDAY LIFE**

PAUL RAWLINS **NO LIE LIKE LOVE**

HARVEY GROSSINGER **THE QUARRY**

HA JIN **UNDER THE RED FLAG**

ANDY PLATTNER **WINTER MONEY**

FRANK SOOS **UNIFIED FIELD THEORY**

CPSIA information can be obtained
at www.ICGtesting.com
Printed in the USA
LVOW08s1007220317
527971LV00004B/23/P